THE SENSE of BLOOD INK

NINE STORIES ABOUT LOVE

The Sense of Blood Ink, an unusual love story, Nick Spill – 1st Edition

nine stories about love

Library of Congress Cataloguing-in-Publication Data

Spill, Nick

Love story – Fiction

Short Story – Fiction

ISBN-13: 979-8-218-12746-6

Book Cover front and back Design: Stewart A. Williams

Photos by author

Format and Design: 52 Novels

More information about Nick Spill's books can be found at
http://nickspill.com
http://nickspill.blogspot.com

THE SENSE of BLOOD INK

NINE STORIES ABOUT LOVE

NICK SPILL

"He who laughs at himself never runs out of things to laugh at."
Epictetus

"Always open with a quote.
It makes you look more intelligent."
Nick Spill

Dedicated to

O, L & U

and
the woman who helped me get through the pandemic
Joy.

CONTENTS

THE SENSE of BLOOD INK

AN UNUSUAL LOVE STORY

"…she is one of the few women who are
once seen and never forgotten."
From *Jacques the Fatalist* by Denis Diderot

CHAPTERS

1

Princess Alexandrina plunged her dagger into Prince Sammanke's chest … the doorbell rang. I leaped out of my chair, dropping my fountain pen.

My study was at the back of a bungalow hidden in a grove of live oak trees down a long driveway in the middle of nowhere, north of the Villages and west of Ocala National Forest. I moved here four years ago after I retired from teaching history to high school kids in Miami and before my third adventure fantasy novel took off. Now my sixth novel was in the bookstores, and I was making a reasonable living as an independent publisher. I planned to sell the film rights for the series. The previous option was about to expire.

The doorbell rang again. The last option met the identical fate as the others. I wasn't expecting a visit from another producer who thought he had discovered the next *Game of Thrones*, only to realize, if he had bothered to read the novels, there were no dragons and little graphic sex, and by little I don't mean little people.

Through the stained glass of the front door, I could see a tall figure with long hair holding something in her right hand. A book? I didn't get unannounced visits. My publishing company was listed as a Delaware Corporation. My website was run by a young fan in Orlando who managed my email list and swore I was untraceable. I wasn't on any social media. My nearest neighbors left me alone. They had probably heard me practicing with my shotgun or pistol in the back garden.

.   .   .

The third ring was followed by three loud knocks. I took my time, still engrossed in what I'd been writing. Did the blade go all the way in? Was there blood oozing onto her hand and dress? I was in another age, another land.

"Who is it?" I asked when I arrived at the double bolted door. The stained design of St. George slaying the dragon was reflected behind hurricane proof glass. My Mossberg 500, loaded with five cartridges and one oo in the tube with the safety on, was hidden in an umbrella stand. I didn't sense any threat.

"My name's Alexandrina Burroughs. I've come to see Zacharias Hideman, who writes under the name of R.H. Hyde."

She had an English accent I couldn't place. Definitely London, but not Cockney and nowhere near Oxford, though her vowels were well defined.

I opened the door on its chain. "How did you find me?"

She held my latest novel, *The Dark Crimson Pilgrimage.*

The name Alexandrina had my attention. She smiled in such a sweet way. I unlatched the chain and opened the door. By this simple action, my life as I knew it would never be the same.

"I bought your book yesterday." She raised it even though I could clearly see the book next to her long legs.

The door was half open and so was my mouth. I'm six foot and dress in khakis, a white shirt, and brown loafers. One of those men who, on waking, shower, shave, and put on a pressed shirt, regardless of my schedule. I needed a haircut, but despite my sedentary lifestyle I was still in shape. I ran my hands through my hair. I wasn't expecting company.

"You gave an interview with a journalist from the Daily Muck, sorry, my name for it, and I know him. I'm in the publishing business and I put two and two together and figured out where you live."

In my life, two and two rarely made four. I was a writer, not a mathematician, so my plots are not predictable. Two and two would make seven or three. "Is this an official visit then?" I was confused as to her presence.

"Oh no. I'm a fan. Pure and simple."

I looked outside before letting her in. My gravel driveway was lined with oak trees and a couple of sabal palms. I spotted a rental car parked to one side. It was facing the house and not blocking my car, tucked away in an open garage on the other side. I turned to face her.

"Then you better come in." Although I had a feeling nothing about this visit would be pure or simple.

She was tall but wore flats, skintight jeans, and a white V-neck T-shirt that showed off her cleavage. Her long black hair was shiny, and she had an English porcelain complexion made pink from the Florida sun she must have caught yesterday. I couldn't make out the color of her eyes, they were too dark to be blue or green. She wore no make-up or lipstick. My character Princess Alexandrina from the *Dark Crimson* series had been transplanted into this century in the middle of Florida, only she had an upturned nose, and her lips were not as full. My Princess Alexandrina had a straight nose and thick, sensuous lips. Not enough difference to make my thoughts more unnerving as I had left my princess with her dagger buried in Prince Sammanke's ribs. My characters inhabited my waking consciousness and sometimes slipped into my dreams, especially when I didn't know what to do with them. But they never invaded my real life.

"Your car?"

"Yes."

"You came alone?'

"Yes. It's just me." She tilted her head to one side.

"And your name is Alexandrina?" I can have difficulty with names, especially when I go for a long time without meeting anyone.

"Yes. I know. It's not why I'm a fan." She walked inside and squatted by two rows of leather-bound books. "Oh my. Your books."

The hallway was lined with bookcases I had built. The entire house seemed to be held up by bookcases crammed with every imaginable type of book.

"*Wind in the Willows*. My favorite,' she said. "How many do you have?"

"I don't want to count them."

She ran her fingers over a row of books of the same name. From where I stood, I could see down her top. I turned away, hoping she wouldn't see me blush. At least I knew she wasn't hiding an edged weapon in her bra.

"I started collecting this one title years ago. Gives me focus when I go to a used bookstore. You never know what you're going to find." I now knew I had to rewrite the last scene, with Alexandrina drawing the dagger from her bodice.

"I love the chapter where Pan appears. The Gates of Dawn. He captures the magic of the English countryside." She knew her Kenneth Grahame.

"Yes, it's very pantheistic, but what I love the most are the action scenes when Badger and Ratty and Mole retake Toad Hall. It's got to be the most violent passage in a children's book because it's so real, let alone Toad being a car thief and cross dressing to break out of prison. It inspired me."

She giggled. "Of course. You have Prince Sammanke dress up as a woman to escape his dungeon in *The Dark Crimson Stones*. That was brilliant."

"No one has ever made the connection before. Maybe I should reread *Willows* to see what else I can find." I walked to the kitchen, she followed, scanning the books on the hallway shelves. Maybe I shouldn't have my Princess kill off Sammanke, although it was a good way to get rid of the sexual tension between them, once and for all. My webmaster, who managed all my social media, online promotions and merchandising had told me there was a lot of speculation about what would happen to them in the next book. He described a Twitter war between Alexandrina's fans, and how violent it became. I found the whole social media affair too far-fetched.

After her last comment how could I not be attracted to her? And physically, she looked stunning in an unpretentious way. Perhaps I felt sexual tension as well if I was being honest with myself.

I took a deep breath and showed her the kitchen, remodeled before I bought the bungalow. It was surprisingly modern compared to the outside. Her eyes took in everything. She looked at home.

"I like to cook." I gestured to the copper pots on the wall and the containers of dried herbs and spices. I had everything in order. "As you probably noticed there are no restaurants around here. Do you want tea?" I put the kettle on, an instinctive reaction to stress. My old English habits coming out. "Take a seat. Fruit cake? Someone sent me a Fortnum and Mason's fruit cake. It's delicious." I got out the tin and started fussing with cups, plates, and a plain white teapot. We were going to have real tea, not American tea bags. "Earl Grey, Royal Blend, or English Breakfast?"

"I'll have what you're having. I can't believe I'm here, sitting with Zacharias Hideman."

"Call me Zach, please. Here, we'll have this. Sent by a fan, I think." I held up an elegant blue tin with the royal gold crest. "Royal Exchange Blend Tea."

"Never seen that one before."

"I still can't believe your name is Alexandrina."

"Yes. I know. It's crazy, isn't it? I was named after my grandmother. Alexandra. But call me Alex."

I dropped the tea strainer, looked at her, blinked, then picked it up and poured the tea as if nothing had happened. Alex didn't seem to notice my agitation. She took her tea black like I did, with no sugar, so no fussing with milk and sugar cubes. I cut her a generous slice of cake to match mine. For some reason I felt as ravenous as I was nervous. We ate in silence, though she did close her eyes and moan as she chewed. I didn't know if this was for my benefit, but it was distracting.

"I didn't catch your last name?" I had finished my cake and had been thinking why she was named after her grandmother.

"Burroughs. Alexandrina Burroughs." She must have caught my frown. "So, the big question is why did you name your heroine Alexandrina? And I apologize if I'm being too personal, but I feel I can talk to you."

I took another deep breath and looked at the teacups.

I had just met this young woman and although I felt a strong connection to her, I was not about to explain how I based my Alexandrina on my first girlfriend, Alexandra. We were teenagers in London. We were madly in love.

I had never told my wife Angela about my first love. As far as Angela had been concerned, *she* was my first love, and nothing was ever going to change that.

Nor could I reveal to Alexandrina what had caused the break-up with my first love. How could I? It was too shameful on reflection. On Saturday afternoons I would visit Alexandra's flat when she was alone, and we would make love. We had been listening to Bob Dylan singing "Lay Lady Lay". I was concentrating on my third time. I was so turned on. And I thought Alexandra was too. She responded to everything I was doing to her. We were naked, in another world. Then she heard her brother enter the flat. She had yelled not to come in, but he had opened her bedroom door without knocking. He froze in the doorway staring at me on top of his sister. Her legs were wrapped around my waist. She got up, dressed and ran to talk to her brother in the living room, while I found my clothes and stumbled into their silent company.

I remember Alexandra had taken me outside her Edwardian building where they rented a flat and told me we couldn't do it anymore, but we could still be friends. She said something about her brother, but I had stopped listening. In my immature mind I took her reaction as an outright rejection, and I stormed off. When I looked back, she was still standing in the street looking bewildered. I think she was crying as she had her hands to her face. I was too consumed with my own pain to consider hers or that we could still be friends in love but not active lovers.

I went to see her a few weeks after we had quarreled. But her family had moved. I searched for her everywhere but couldn't find her. I never saw her again.

.   .   .

"To answer your question. I once knew a girl called Alexandra. I think she lived in NW 10. You know?" I shrugged and hid my hands under the table.

"I know the area. Willesden?"

"Yes. I went back there with my wife, about 10 years ago. It had changed a lot."

"London is constantly changing. That's what makes it such a fascinating place to live."

"Are you echoing Samuel Johnson?" I attempted to smile, pleased to change the subject.

She nodded.

"What was the Virginia Woolf quote the journalist used?" I asked. "That was a nice sidebar on Virginia Wolff and her full size wax figure in my old college."

"*London itself perpetually attracts, stimulates, gives me a play and a story and a poem.* At least he got the quote right. I still don't get why he picked Virginia Woolf to compare you to."

"Me neither. I'm not exactly in the same league as her, am I?"

"I didn't mean it like that, Zach."

"I'd forgotten the quote. And I've no idea either why he included her other than we both went to the same King's College."

"That was it. And he had to fill up space. Writing about Woolf is free. Her lifelike wax sculpture in a, what would you call it, a cupboard, is extraordinary, isn't it?"

"Yes. I'll have to visit next time I'm in London. Maybe I'll write about it and call the article 'A Castle of my Own.'"

She laughed at the allusion to Woolf's *A Room of My Own*.

"But we do have a shameful press. As you know from seeing that journalist."

"Oh god! You called it the Daily Muck? It is. And that journalist who interviewed me? How well did you know him?"

"Not that well. At least he told me how to get to your place, otherwise I would never have found you."

"What did he tell you?"

"He drew me a map on a napkin in a bar. He was very drunk. I never saw him again."

"Put me off doing any more interviews. I knew there was something odd about him. He even admitted he talked his editor into interviewing me so he could visit Disney."

Here I was having a perfectly civil conversation with a real life Alexandrina. I couldn't get over the similarities to Princess Alexandrina, her facial expressions, the way she threw her hair back. I was intrigued, wary, nervous, and most of all, curious. "So, you're not called Drina? Like Queen Victoria?"

"Oh no. My mother tried but I stopped her." She smiled.

I was trying to understand why such a gorgeous young woman would appear unannounced at my house, miles away from anywhere. Yet here she was in my kitchen, examining everything.

Six novels and no stalkers, only one unannounced fan visit. Was this normal? The next fantasy convention I attended I would ask the other writers, although I didn't trust them to tell the truth. At the last convention, conveniently held in Orlando, I was told you're not famous until you have at least one stalker. I didn't think Alexandrina counted as a stalker.

She refused another piece of cake and patted her lips with the paper napkin I had given her.

"You've got a little crumb here." I pointed to the tip of my nose and noted Alexandrina did not have an upturned nose as I first observed. Maybe it was how she sat now, but her nose looked perfect along with her entire face. I tried not to stare as she brushed her napkin over her straight nose.

"Perfect."

She looked at me, a serious expression on her face.

"What I like about your writing, and this makes you stand out from other fantasy writers, is you don't spell everything out. It's what's not said that's important. That's how you build tension and suspense. So many writers believe they should explain every action and thought. But with you the reader has to work to understand what's going on. What used to be called subtext, the currents flowing under the surface. You get it, so the informed reader goes along with your style of writing."

"Well, thank you. The critics, whom I don't read, say I'm opaque, or obtuse, or plain lazy, and don't describe what's going on with the characters. So … …." I clapped my hands then felt silly for the outward display of emotion and didn't know what to say next. She might question how I knew what critics said about my work if I claimed not to read them. But she didn't respond to my humor.

"It's as if you deliberately withhold information from the reader: the main character in the scene knows what's going on but her rival doesn't and nor do we. It's a mean trick, even in literary terms."

"It's not *as if*, it *is*. And yes, it works."

"Zach, I mean the reader has to work harder." Alex started to play with her hair, and she caught me staring at her hands. She let her hair fall behind her shoulders.

I tried not to shiver and looked out the kitchen window to the magnolia tree.

"I never knew I was a fantasy writer until the label was hoisted on me. I'm just a writer telling a story. A good story I hope."

I was starting to doubt my ability as a writer with powers of observation as I watched Alex. The way her body moved, her eyes, her hair, everything about her seemed to contradict her controlled voice. Her body was reacting in a different way from what she was saying, and I could not read her let alone understand what was happening.

"With a bag of tricks." She smiled. And I wondered who really had the bag of tricks.

"Why do you say that? Technique, please, not tricks."

"Zach, I love the way you write. One of the reasons why I'm a fan." She gave me a big smile and got up from her chair to help me put things away. She looked at the floor and out the window again before she turned to me.

"You don't have cats or dogs? Why no animals?"

I pulled a face. Who had I let into my house? First, I was confused about her and didn't know if she was teasing me or not and now, she was asking me why I didn't have any animals?

"What I mean is your books are full of animals, giant dogs and fierce cats. And let's not forget the horses."

I wanted to forget horses, unless they were in my books. When I met my wife, she had her own horse, a chestnut mare. I was on vacation in Miami after I had graduated from King's College in London. I had a master's in history, not the first class honors I had strived for, and I was confronted with how to make a living. I didn't want to teach at London University, despite a research offer with very low pay. So, I jumped on a plane, rented a car and stayed at a cheap hotel on Miami Beach. On my second day I got lost. I was going to the Everglades to see the sea of grass and alligators, but instead I wound up at a Farmer's store in Davie. I watched a very pretty blonde in a cowboy hat and boots tie her horse to a hitching post and walk into the store. By the time I had parked, she was outside, drinking a soda and feeding her horse an apple. Somehow, I lost my shyness and started talking to her.

I have no idea what I said, but she later mythologized our first meeting. She used to tell it at parties, especially to her girlfriends. She was taken by my English accent; I was intrigued by her white teeth and raucous laugh. We talked outside the store for what seemed like hours, but it was only a few minutes. There was something between us that clicked. Even her horse seemed to like me, especially as I ran into the store and bought another apple. I followed Angela on her horse in my car, to her stables. After more discussion, I drove her to Miami Beach where we ate at a Jewish diner, and I fell in love with the food. I liked to tell that side of the story, rather than falling in love with Angela. I drove her back to her parents' horse farm. We stayed talking on a swing on her veranda for the rest of the night, and I got lost again returning to my hotel. I remember parking by the beach walking on the sand barefoot. I was filled with emotions I didn't understand as I witnessed the sun rise over the Atlantic Ocean. We saw each other every day until I flew back, but not until I had applied for a teaching position with the local School Board who were desperate for teachers.

I got a phone call the next week and they wanted me to start immediately. They thought King's College was in Oxford, and I was highly qualified to teach history. That was how I came to live in South Florida. And of course, I knew nothing about American history.

Angela had been mad about horses. I couldn't bear to see them now, though they existed in my books as definable characters. I didn't know where to go from here with Alex. I didn't want to explain my wife to her.

"I'm sorry if that was too personal a question."

She must have read the expression on my face.

"Do you have a cat or dog?" I deflected.

"One cat. A tuxedo. I took him to my father's place in Norfolk last weekend. Didn't want to leave him alone in my flat."

"After my rottweiler died in Miami I swore I would never own another dog. And cats here, well, they'd play havoc with the birds. There's a raven who visits me, but he's far from the ravens in my books. What do you call your tuxedo?"

"Pierre, from *War and Peace*. He's a very Chelsea cat. And I didn't name him anything like Clawdrina. Where did you get that name?"

"Thought it was obvious. Alexandrina with claws. A cross between a panther and a large domestic cat. It's an imaginary world, so I played around and gave her magical powers. I even have a company that produces T-shirts with the animals and characters. Still not happy with the depiction of Alexandrina though."

"Do you have her image etched in your mind?" She made a face as if she knew the answer.

I wanted to say, *I do now*. Instead, I bit my tongue and lowered my eyes. I took a deep breath and saw she was still looking at me.

"We all have different ways of seeing people." It seemed a diplomatic response. I could hardly confess that I was spellbound by her likeness to Princess Alexandrina. "And the animals, I've gotten such a strong response to her cat."

"I imagined I'd be greeted by giant guard dogs when I drove up."

"Sorry to disappoint you. I wanted to call them dragon hounds but the allusion to *The Song of Ice and Fire* books was too close. I admire George Martin though, and in a way he's a model for all fantasy writers that follow him, but I wanted to be different."

"And the dogs of truth?"

"Actually, they're the Hounds of Truth, like the dogs of war. Handy dealing with traitors. You can see here, no fences, no gates. Another reason I don't want dogs." I didn't want to talk about my former dog, or the cats I had left behind in the house I had sold when I moved here.

I folded the tea towel and tucked it into the roller. I had refused to turn my animals into tea towel designs. And I didn't want to get into a discussion about my merchandising. My webmaster had produced amazing designs from my *Dark Crimson* world. We sold them on T-shirts and other clothing and products. He was paid an attractive commission on sales, so he was highly motivated and almost earned as much as I did from my writing. They sold well on the website and at conventions. Bookstores were ordering them as well. Weren't they supposed to sell books? I was amazed how many non-book items were being pushed in bookstores now. Didn't anyone read? It was a consolation that I had a live reader and fan in my house. A consolation that confounded me. But I had in mind what my late wife Angela said about good taste. I shook off thoughts of the Hounds of Truth on tea towels and turned to my guest.

"You said you live in Chelsea?"

"Yes."

"Posh."

"I inherited the flat from my auntie. A gorgeous location. I love it there."

I nodded. Every time I returned to London I had been with my Angela, and I didn't want to bring up memories of her. She adored England and was in love with London.

"Do you want a tour of the house? Is that what I'm supposed to do now?" This was the longest conversation I'd had with a stranger for a long time, and I felt exposed. I had a poet friend, another retired teacher, who lived a few miles away. She was fun to visit and always had incense burning. She wore flowing robes, had long silver hair she refused to dye, and a house full of cats. Her hallway was lined with prints from *The Kama Sutra,* and she played sitar music whenever I came over. I went for weeks without seeing her, but she was always delighted to see me. I would listen to her latest poem and drink her wine, but we were strictly platonic, I think.

I stood outside my bedroom door at the rear of the house and cleared my throat. The door was ajar, but I had no intention of entering. "My bedroom. It was redone along with the kitchen." I wasn't going to show her the giant freestanding bathtub or the rainfall shower. "And here's the spare bedroom, which has its own bathroom." I barely opened the door so she could peek in. For a moment, I had a vision of her staying here. I blocked the thought. "In front here is what I call my relaxation room. See, no bookcases."

On the coffee table were a pile of oversized illustrated books about armory, siege machines, and medieval history. The only place you could sit was on a large sofa. On either side of a brick fireplace were giant speakers and in the corner were an array of older sound equipment, amps with valves, an ancient CD player, a top of the line turntable and racks of albums in red milk crates. "This is where I chill out at night. Listen to jazz." I must have moved my shoulders because she inched a little closer to me. I took a step back.

"But what you really want to see is this." I strode down the hallway a little too quickly and swung open the wooden door to my study, the biggest room in the house. The space had been the back porch before the house was remodeled. A large window looked out on my vegetable and flower gardens and a small orchard. In the distance a clump of trees marked the boundary of my property, live oak, red maple, and dogwood. A mature magnolia tree stood on its own, which in spring would be surrounded by azaleas. In the shade I had assembled a wooden bench and table, with a patch of grass in front.

Two walls had floor to ceiling bookcases I had installed, and the other wall was pinned with maps, a giant whiteboard covered with names, dates and drawings and another board with a timetable and names of characters in neat rows. I pointed to two wooden desks side by side facing the window and noticed my fountain pen on the floor. I bent down to pick it up, inspected the nib and screwed the cap on. I looked at her, and she didn't say anything. She couldn't have been a fountain pen enthusiast as she would have commented on the Montblanc Meisterstück pen, the gold nib, or the snowcap emblem.

"I write a lot of my ideas and dialogue in my notebooks. Then I rewrite on my laptop. And sometimes the other way round. Excuse the mess, but I've been trying to work out what happens in the seventh and final book."

"Oh, so it's true. There's only one more. I wish it would go on forever."

"They might but I'm not."

"Oh no, are you ill?" She sounded concerned.

"No." I laughed. "Not at all. I want to write something else. These characters have been with me such a long time."

"Can you sign my book? Wherever it is."

"You left it in the kitchen."

"And you want to get rid of all the characters?"

"I didn't say that. And it might be I can't resolve everything. It's not my style anyway, so I can always come back to the storyline later." I turned to her. She stood close to me. "I'm still trying to process your name." I could not stop thinking about her name, her unexpected visit, the way she looked compared to my central character. I am obsessive, weren't writers supposed to be obsessive? It was how I got the story out of my subconscious. I was always thinking of my writing.

"Yes. When I first came across Princess Alexandrina in *The Dark Crimson Stones*, you were describing me. It was like I had suddenly come alive and could see myself as I had never seen myself before. Do you understand?"

I nodded, but I didn't understand what was happening. In my books, there were no coincidences. Everything happened for a purpose, even if it wasn't revealed for several chapters or until the next book. I tried to connect every plot line, so standing here looking at Alexandrina and how she resembled my fictional heroine made me nervous.

She had already said at afternoon tea I left some matters unsaid. The reader had to work out what was going on. I wasn't going to voice any of the emotions whirling around inside me.

I watched her as she absorbed all the details in the room, to a point where I felt I was being spied on.

"What did you say you do in publishing?"

"I work as a proofreader and junior editor, which means I do odd jobs from making coffee or tea to buying magazines and newspapers. I got a Ph.D. in philosophy. Turned out to be pretty useless but pleased my parents as they call me Doctor."

"Should I call you Dr. Alex?"

"Please, no. It's so pretentious. Who cares about the Greeks anymore? We should, but we don't."

She saw copies of my books on the shelf. "*The Dark Crimson Stones, The Dark Crimson Battlefield, The Dark Crimson Tree of Death*, my favorite. You go all out in *The Dark Crimson Sword of Life, The Dark Crimson Curse* and yes, what I'm looking forward to, *Pilgrimage*." She gasped and sounded like a real fan. She saw the title to my final book at the top of a whiteboard. "Is this the last one? *The Dark Crimson Revelation*? It does sound final." She put her hands to her ears. "Don't tell me what it's about. Don't spoil it."

"I need copies so I can refer to passages, details I need to remind myself about. As you can see, I try to keep track of all the story points." I waved my hand at the board, and she ran her eyes over the names and my writing. I wasn't going to tell her I had no idea what was going to happen in *Revelation*. "I have extra copies of all my books in a special bookshelf in the other room. I've got boxes of them. Do you want a set?"

She turned around to face me.

"You're very generous. But I didn't come here to get books. I wanted to see you."

"Well, you got the ten-cent tour, or should I say one shilling?" I smiled. I wasn't sure if she got the joke. Without thinking I asked, "When are you leaving?" It seemed like a good question. I trusted she didn't think she was moving in. Though I had no idea what she was thinking. She gave me a look of disappointment. Angela used to give me the same look if I hadn't lived up to her expectations, as in "You're not going out in that shirt, are you?" I should have known the correct response: "Of course not, darling, I didn't want to get the new shirt you bought me dirty while I take out the garbage."

Alex was silent for some time. We were still in my study, and I was relieved she hadn't sat down, anywhere. Least of all on the sofa. It was on the sofa I daydreamed about my Princess Alexandrina, something I wanted to keep to myself.

"Do you want me to leave now? I can if you want. The last thing I want to do is make you feel uncomfortable."

"No, no. I just wanted to know your plans."

"I'm on holiday and have no plans other than catching a plane back to Heathrow in ten days' time."

I wondered if she noticed how I flinched at the mention of ten days. Was she moving in?

"What did you do when you arrived? Orlando, right?"

"Yes. I went to Disney yesterday. Well, I think I saw one park, as they're called. Had an amazing chocolate ice cream, but I'm not a Disney fan. It was all bars and shops and badly dressed people waddling about. So, I drove to Winter Park. I'd heard it was different from Orlando and I stumbled on a bookstore, and you'd never guess what was in the window."

"*Pilgrimage.*"

"How did you know?"

"I did a reading, no two readings there. Have they sold out again?"

"I bought the last one."

"Great store. What did you do after?"

"I went back to my hotel and walked over to another park and heard some jazz last night. Never expected to hear live music."

"What jazz do you like?"

"Anything not contemporary. I hate all this easy listening jazz. Give me Lester Young, Cannonball Adderley, Charlie Parker, or early Miles Davis."

"I have those albums," I let slip out. It was almost an invitation to stay, soak in jazz, sip whisky, sit by the fire. January was cold at night here in central Florida.

"Oh, I'd love to hear some jazz. I can still hear those Disney songs. They play endlessly."

She took a deep breath, lowered her chin, fixed me with her eyes then closed her eyelids for a second before gazing at me. I had described Princess Alexandrina perform similar movements when she was not getting what she wanted in court, and I wanted to grab one of my books and find the passage. But this, for now, seemed a bad idea, as did asking her if she was copying Princess Alexandrina's expression or if she did this naturally.

"Do you have plans to see more of Florida?"

"I'm open." She used her eye trick again.

It was my cue to come up with a plan. So far, my encounter with Alex had been innocent. I had no intentions, good, bad, erotic, neurotic or otherwise. Here was a perfectly beautiful young fan who had fallen out of the sky to spend time with me, and I should be enjoying myself, not overthinking the plot, as if we were in one of my novels. I was unsure what to do. I wanted to be the perfect host and accord her all the courtesies an unannounced princess would receive in one of my books. I also wanted to see her out the door and, on her way, but I could not banish her from my house, as there was something about her I found intriguing. No, that was not the right word. Attractive? Of course. But there was something else I could not put my finger on. She had provided me enough clues, innocent or not, but I refused to see them.

I resolved I should try to get to know her better, rather than get rid of her. How often does a beautiful young woman knock on my door? And bearing the name of my heroine? I took a deep breath and changed my tone.

"I know a lovely spot not far from here. There's a river, slow moving, well, more like a lake, hopefully not too many bugs for this time of year and usually no one else is around. We could take a picnic, an early dinner, drinks, watch the trees, the clouds, maybe some birds. I can put something together now?"

"Let me help you."

Alex followed me to the kitchen, then into the garden as I picked a lettuce and a few tomatoes from my greenhouse.

"I don't know how I lived before I made this. It's small but very productive. Are you a vegetarian?" I asked.

"No. I'll eat anything other than pork and shellfish."

I should've picked up on what she said, but my mind was elsewhere.

"I have a loaf of bread I baked yesterday, some cheese and we can make a salad. Wine?"

"Oh yes. You've got to be able to drink huge quantities of wine if you work in publishing in London."

"Really? Is it still a pub culture?"

"It's sort of evolved, but yes, young women drink, a lot. If you can't hold your drink, you get called names."

"Well, I have no one to call me names, but I've cut back on my drinking. I stopped sipping whisky when I'm alone. It seemed like a bad habit."

"I stopped drinking wine alone too." She patted her midriff.

For the first time I noticed her flat stomach. She looked in great shape. My mind started to wander to my main character again and her dagger. I headed to a closet in the hallway and found a large blanket and cushions and my wicker picnic hamper someone sent me from F&M. The hamper came from another film producer who had not read my books but was courting me for the film rights.

She helped me pack everything and it seemed natural like we had been together for ages. Before we left, she turned to me. I must have appeared flustered, and for a moment she looked like she was going to kiss me on the cheek but decided against it. Did she see the brief panic in my eyes?

"You might want to take a jacket; it'll get colder once the sun goes down."

I grabbed my car keys by the front door, and a sweater. We walked to the side of the house where I kept my prized possession, a reward I gave myself after last year's record sales. A Dodge Challenger SRT 392. A 6.4-liter V8 engine. A muscle car in battleship gray.

The engine purred in neutral as I stopped by her car, and she picked up her leather jacket from her back seat. She slid into my car again and looked at home. When I tapped the accelerator, I could feel the eight cylinders come to life. Alex squirmed in her seat, reacting to the power, the throbbing engine, the vibrations. If I knew her better and was more daring, I would've said something. Instead, I shot her an anemic smile. I've never caught a speeding ticket. I had the power but had no need to show off. It helped I befriended the local sheriff when I first moved here: contributed to his reelection then donated more money so he could install a big screen monitor in his office. I had his personal cell, but half the county probably did.

I told Alex how I'd been a teacher then became a full-time writer and found my house. If she had read the article, she would've known about Angela dying of cancer and my new life as a widower, after thirty years of marriage. Although now I was thinking of myself as a single man with an attractive woman next to me in my muscle car. I shook my head, concentrated on my driving and recounted to Alex my adventures trying to sell the film rights to the series.

"Oh my god! I can see the books as an epic adventure series on Amazon or Netflix. It would be brilliant."

"It's finding the right people who can sell the idea to the right people. So far, I've gone through two producers. I sold the option for six months the last time and it's about to expire. Perhaps next time I'll hire a big-time entertainment lawyer to negotiate, for its all a mystery to me, the whole process. I'm just a writer."

"Zach, you're more than that," she murmured.

I was saved from reacting to the last remark when I took an unmarked turn and had to maneuver my way down a bumpy, narrow lane, where, at the end, we arrived at a deserted riverbank.

We walked to an ideal picnic spot. She laid out the blanket and pillows, sat cross legged, adjusted her hair, and gazed at me. She looked serene. I bent over to open the basket then put my sweater on. Alex didn't seem to mind the cold.

"All we need now are willows." She laughed.

"And Ratty and Mole in a boat. Too much! Here, let's eat. I don't know why I'm starving."

She stood and looked across the still water.

"Join me for a swim. We don't need clothes here, right?" She was about to pull off her T-shirt as she turned to me. She stopped when I shook my finger.

"Alligators. There are always alligators in these waters and it's breeding season. The males can be very aggressive."

She froze, then adjusted her T-shirt as she turned to scan the water. "I don't see any."

"You wouldn't. They sneak up on you underwater and drag you down. But don't worry, they won't disturb us on dry ground."

Alex sat cross legged and turned her attention to the food. Throughout our picnic she continued to scan the water.

She served the salad, grapes, bread, and cheese, while I poured the Sancerre I had selected from my modest wine collection. When I bought the house, it came with a small wine refrigerator, which I kept well stocked.

"How long have you lived here?"

"Four years. I don't think that was in the article. It's quiet here and I can work uninterrupted. I'd never have been able to produce a book a year in Miami."

"Do you get many visitors?"

"Not that many."

"What do you mean?"

"Well, I have a woman come once a week to clean the house and do the laundry. Got a few locals who call me or invite me over for dinner. I know more people back in England than I do here. And you don't usually walk up to someone's house unannounced. They're all armed."

She shivered.

"Guns, alligators, muscle cars. Florida must seem a weird place," I countered.

"And don't forget Mickey," she threw back at me.

I laughed.

She smiled and sipped her wine, looking at the water then back at me.

I offered her the last of the grapes; she shook her head, and I finished them.

After watching me for some time, she asked, "Zach, do you get lonely?"

I tried not to frown. Where was this going? Was I over-thinking our encounter? I had to go with my gut instinct. The trouble was my gut was telling me something entirely opposite from what my common sense was screaming.

"I have all my characters, the next book to occupy me."

"If I hadn't knocked on your door would you be working on the seventh one now?"

"I'm enjoying the break." I finished my wine and looked at her again, completely frown free. "Tell me more about yourself. I feel like I'm out of touch with meeting new people. It's never the same with conventions or book readings. What about your family? You mentioned your parents. Are you close?"

"I was close to my mother. But she died two years ago. Cancer. Like your wife. I was closer to my aunt who left me her flat. She was Jewish. I know my mother was, but she wasn't religious."

"Oh, I'm sorry. Was your aunt orthodox?"

"Well, she observed the holidays, lit candles on Friday night. She made me promise I would bring up my children Jewish."

"Oh. So that's why you don't eat pork or shellfish?"

"Yes, I suppose so. It was a clue." She smiled.

"What about your father? Is he Jewish?"

"No, he isn't. After my mother died, he became emotionally remote and moved to Norfolk. I try to see him as much as I can, but it's difficult. Maybe the cat will cheer him up."

"Any brothers or sisters?"

"I was an only child. I became a tomboy."

"Tomboy? That's a word I haven't heard in a long time. I can't imagine you as a tomboy."

"Climbing trees, fighting boys, beating them at cricket and tennis. Then I started growing up and reading books. Lots of books."

"Nothing wrong with reading a lot. I'm eternally thankful to all who read my books. They're long, involved and have intricate plots. I have to reread the last one before I start on my next."

"That's funny. Don't you have everything in your head?"

"You'd be surprised how little is in my head."

"I don't believe you. I've seen some of your recorded readings. You're very sexy. Don't you get women knocking on your hotel room at night? Fans stalking you?"

"Not hotel rooms. Only my house. And you're my first stalker."

"I'm not a stalker. Am I? Do you think I'm a stalker?" She sat upright and for a moment she was dead serious. She turned to scan the water again.

"Not at all. I'm teasing you. I feel comfortable with you if you want to know."

Comfortable was a slight exaggeration. She had just described me as sexy. The last word I would've used to describe myself. Should I have been flattered or alarmed? Probably both. I didn't tell her that at conventions I never stayed at the hotel where it was held but at an unassuming place further away and under another name.

"Good, because you know, Zach, I feel comfortable with you too. Especially as I've drunk half a bottle of wine and feel a little tipsy."

"Eat some more of this bread. It'll help." There was that word we had used. Comfortable. "Besides, you're much too thin."

She placed a hand on her stomach, glanced at her midriff, then at me. "You're teasing me again."

I raised my eyebrows and kept my position on the blanket. If I was writing a romance, this was where I would lean over and kiss her, first gently, no hands, then holding her neck, followed by a passionate kiss lasting longer than a Chopin étude. Although I don't think Chopin would work in the middle of Florida next to a lake full of imaginary alligators and real mosquitoes.

"There's a mosquito on your face. There." I pointed. She whacked her left cheek and left a bloody mark from the mosquito. "It's time to leave."

She didn't say much on the journey home other than peek every few minutes at her lighted visor mirror to check the red mark on her cheek.

"They must love your fresh English blood."

She pouted her lips.

"I take it you checked out of your hotel in Orlando?"

"Yes."

I stole a glance at her and for a moment thought she looked guilty. It would be good to apply the way she used her eyes and lips in a scene with Princess Alexandrina.

"Would you like to stay the night? You've had a lot to drink and shouldn't drive in the dark on these roads. My spare room's available."

"That's very sweet of you." She leaned back in her seat; her eyes fixed on me. Had she planned to stay with me all along?

"I can light a fire, play some jazz and maybe have a drink."

"Yes, sounds lovely. You have no idea what it's like being in some anonymous hotel room with a lumpy mattress and smelly drapes."

"I do actually. And the outrageous minibar prices. Do you have your suitcase in your car?"

"Yes. In the boot. I'll get it."

"I haven't heard that word in ages."

She looked at me again.

"Boot." I repeated.

"What do you say?"

"Trunk."

"But that's a large suitcase," she protested and laughed.

I could get used to her laugh.

I showed her the spare bedroom and bathroom and gave her a special ointment for her insect bite. I noticed she had a twig stuck in the back of her hair but decided not to say anything.

In the kitchen, I knocked back the remains of the Sancerre then went to light the fire. I placed my favorite Lester Young album on the turntable. Back in the kitchen I found two Baccarat glasses but put them back in the cupboard. Angela loved those, and I wasn't ready to use them. I found a couple of cut glasses, the kind you get in a promotion when you buy a special bottle. I poured two generous bourbons, no ice.

She had freshened up and sat next to me on a cushion, her back to the sofa. I liked sitting on the floor to stare at the fire. I didn't have a TV. My fire was my TV. Once I finished the *Dark Crimson* series, I'd think about getting a TV. For now, I didn't need one. She leaned over to me as she sipped her drink.

"Did you mean it about the alligators? Or were you trying to stop me taking off my clothes?"

"Things always go wrong in my books. I didn't want anything to happen to you."

Alex looked at me, then after a pause, she commented how warm the bourbon felt inside her as she held it to the light of the fire.

"You know I'm twenty-nine."

I held up my glass to the fire and saw the amber liquid shake. "You look younger but act older, and I'm a poor judge of age."

"Thank you. I broke up with my boyfriend recently. We'd been together for a long time."

"I'm sorry." Was I? It seemed the right thing to say. "Why the break-up?" I asked. She wasn't forthcoming with an answer, and I could see her eyelids starting to lower. She shook her head and looked at me.

"It wasn't working out. He wasn't committed to me, so I'm single again." She sighed.

"Here's to being single." I raised my glass, and she clinked her glass against mine.

We listened to the rich tenor saxophone. Her head came to rest on my shoulder, and she started to snore, like a rabbit. Although technically I've never heard a rabbit snore, she did sound cute, and vulnerable. I had to admit I enjoyed her company. The fire died out and I didn't want to replenish the logs and wake her. In the silence after the album, she opened her eyes and took a moment to collect herself. I swallowed the bourbon I had left in my glass.

I escorted her to the spare bedroom, mentioned the towels in her bathroom, then closed her door. No good-night kiss on the check or any hint of intimacy. I didn't see myself as timid but now was not the time. I could've held her when she rested on my shoulder. I imagined she expected me to. But I didn't want to start something, whatever that something was.

Living alone in the middle of nowhere I had a routine where I checked the house was secure. I tidied the kitchen, ran the dishwasher, raked the fire and made sure the screen was closed before going to bed. I shut the door to my bedroom. None of the inside doors had locks on them. After washing my face and brushing my teeth I put on a clean pair of pajamas and slipped into my queen size bed. I tried to recount my most unusual day. Images of my real guest who was in the bed in the next room swirled around with the equally real fictional heroine of my books. The bourbon made my head spin.

When I published a new novel, I obsessed over the stats for the first month. I would check my sales figures on Amazon late at night. Last night I saw *Pilgrimage* was doing far better than the other novels had after their launch. I knew I had a hit on my hands. My webmaster and I had organized the launch party and reading in Winter Park. There were lines down the street for fans who wanted to buy a personally inscribed copy of *The Dark Crimson Pilgrimage*. The store sold all the copies they had ordered as well as the remaining copies of my other five books. And let's not forget all the T-shirts and other merchandise. I had to return and do another round of signing which I was delighted to do. My webmaster claimed the online promotion made it a success and I was compelled to sign T-shirts if they bought the book as well.

I loved to hear from genuine readers who were devoted to my work and asked interesting questions. Of course, the one question I got asked the most was who I modeled Princess Alexandrina's character on. I was told she was too real to be completely made up. That I must have been inspired by a very special woman. The more preceptive readers asked if she was the love of my life who escaped me. There was no straight answer to these questions for I would've had to admit something from my past I was not proud of. The real Alexandrina was asleep in the next room, and I hadn't even kissed her goodnight.

2

The way she stood in the doorway, I could see the gap between her thighs, backlit by the light from the hall. Then I noticed she was wearing one of my pajama tops, an old one, the stripes faded and some buttons missing. She leaned against the door jamb as she scrutinized me with an expression I couldn't decipher. When she breathed in, the top lifted enough for me to see she wasn't wearing underwear and the bra she had worn the day before hadn't been padded.

"Where did you find that?" I surprised myself with a full sentence before my first coffee.

"It was under the pillow."

I wanted to groan but kept quiet. She reminded me of a Playboy model, posing with her long legs.

Before I met my Angela I used to read or rather pore over *Playboy* magazines. Now I fantasized over my princess. I was consumed with my characters to such a degree that although I was alone, I never felt lonely.

Staring at Alex, I did feel lonely. I had no one in my life I cared about.

"Do you want me to join you?"

"Too big a question so early in the morning." I had my hands on top of the sheet across my chest.

She pouted, and I saw a gleam of disappointment in her face.

"Well, sit at the end of the bed." I pointed to where my feet were.

Alex, eyes fixed on me, sat cross legged at the foot of the bed. I moved my feet to make room for her and accidentally confirmed she wore no underwear.

"I came to check on you during the night. I wondered what the noise was. It was you snoring. I could hear you in my room."

I had an image of her standing over my bed while I was in a deep sleep. I felt very uncomfortable. There was no way I was going to enter into any type of intimacy with a desirable woman I had known for less than twenty-four hours.

Was she parting her legs a little as she followed my gaze?

I let out a deep sigh. "Let's have breakfast. Oatmeal? Eggs and toast? And lots of coffee."

She was thrown off by my lack of interest in her. I think. I was still trying to understand her and wondered if my imagination was playing tricks on me as to her intentions. I was a widower, didn't date, and had no desire to start an affair with another woman. My wife had made me promise I would date and remarry, or at least have a long-term relationship with someone, someone to look after me. I remember Angela's words. I had to swear I would try, but I didn't have the heart to go out and be with other women. Living in a remote spot in the middle of Florida didn't help my chances of getting a date for Saturday night. I wasn't on any social media and my online presence was limited to my website, managed remotely. Alex was the first woman who had slept over and much as I was enjoying the experience, I was still unnerved by her, the way she acted like one of my created characters. Then there was the age difference.

Thirty years seemed too great a gap, but I kept my thoughts to myself. Coffee and oatmeal would make me feel better.

"If you'll excuse me, I'll get dressed." I didn't watch her exit my bedroom as I made a run for my bathroom.

.   .   .

Alex appeared in the kitchen. In tight jeans and a white long sleeved shirt tailored to fit her body, she wore no make-up or jewelry, and she looked spectacular. I served her oatmeal from the pot together with a mug of hot coffee. Alex positioned the honey bottle over her oatmeal and squeezed with a powerful grip, while staring at me. The plastic bottle seemed to collapse on itself. So did I.

"Do you like the honey? It's from a local beekeeper." I ignored my demolished bottle.

"It's good," she murmured as she concentrated on her oatmeal and occasionally looked at me as I returned her gaze.

"No cell phone? No photos?" I was under the impression the younger generation was obsessed with their phones and selfies. Everywhere I went in Orlando I saw such behavior.

"I'm on vacation."

If I knew her better, I would have detected not what I took to be veiled hostility but a reticence to explain why she wasn't using her cell phone, which I'm sure she was never without in London. I raised the French press, and she nodded yes. I poured more coffee.

"There isn't anyone I want to talk to. Besides, there's you." She batted her eyelids. "And you'd throw me out if I was on my phone."

I grunted and started to clear away the dishes. There was that stated dare, would I throw her out? I wanted her to stay, at least for another day. Much as I was wary of her and her sudden presence in my life, I was also intrigued and, dare I admit, very attracted to her.

.   .   .

After breakfast we walked around the garden and inspected the fruit trees. I showed her where I had installed an additional water pump for the garden, my irrigation hoses, and the small greenhouse again. Wildflowers that I'd either planted or encouraged grew in clusters around the property, including black medic and crimson clover. I loved the allusions to my novels. The air was cool but warm enough for bees and there was a slight breeze. I pointed out a red cardinal and several other birds Alex hadn't seen before.

"Do you like gardens?"

"I adore English gardens. It's so peaceful strolling through them. Promise me we can have tea outside here at your table under the magnolia."

"It's a deal. But first let me take you to a place I've been wanting to go to but never had anyone to take."

"Oh, that's so sad." She touched my arm and I presumed she wasn't kidding me. It did sound pathetic, but when it came to my personal life, which was nonexistent, I was pathetic.

.   .   .

Back in my study I searched my laptop and showed her the results as she leaned over me. I could feel her breast press against my shoulder through her cotton shirt but ignored it. I caught an article about a new flu epidemic but chose to ignore that as well. I rarely followed the news online. I stopped reading newspapers a long time ago and with no TV I was thankfully not exposed to mainstream media.

"Bok Tower Gardens. It's about a ninety-minute drive down Route 27 and we can avoid Orlando and Disney traffic. Also, you'll see a part of Florida you wouldn't normally see."

"You mean rednecks and the Klan?"

"No. God forbid. Actually, we'll be near Lakeland, the Frank Lloyd Wright designed university. Or we can head over to Tampa. I know a great restaurant there. Let's go there after. Better take something more formal to wear. I'm taking a tie and a jacket, just in case. Bern's is my favorite steakhouse. They grow and age the beef themselves, and you can see fresh fish swimming in their giant aquarium in their kitchen."

"No. An aquarium inside a kitchen? Only in America."

"Yes, only in America. The English don't think like that do they?"

"Zach, do you think of yourself as English? Or are you American now?"

"Dual citizen. When I'm cut, I bleed red, white, and blue."

"So, you go both ways?" She leaned her head on my shoulder and her hair drifted across my face. I found the sensation captivating. I closed my eyes and tried to breath normally. I couldn't tell if she was teasing or taunting me. Truth be told, I wouldn't know the difference. I decided not to answer her. I eased up from my chair, so I no longer had anything pressed into my shoulder.

.   .   .

Alex threw a small bag into the back of the Challenger with her leather jacket and a hat. She had put on her sunglasses. She did look striking, either fully dressed or in my pajama top.

"You have sunscreen for your tan and a hat? The sun is unusually strong here, which I take you found out?"

"Yes. Hence the long sleeved shirt." She ran her hands down to her cuffs and I noticed how the cotton clung to her body and the buttons looked as if they were held together by magic. I touched the accelerator and the V8 throbbed with suppressed power as we cruised up my driveway. She looked like she was melting into her seat.

I stopped at the mailbox, a giant milk can with my number painted on the side, at the main road and retrieved a large brown envelope.

"I have a PO box in Miami, and they forward my mail every week. Not many people know where I live. It's listed under a corporation, and gives me an extra layer of security, even though you can find my name misspelled in the local property website." I turned to her before I launched the car south. She was flung back in her seat and gave a little yelp then lowered her sunglasses to throw me a puzzled look. I eased off the throttle.

I took a short detour, and we came to a fast moving road with two lanes on either side.

"Is this Route 27? Like Route 66?"

"I don't think you'd get your kicks here." I turned to Alex and smiled. She nodded her head.

41

"Goes all the way to Bok Tower. Better than taking I-75. Get to see a little of America. Florida."

"It's all built up. I was expecting more open spaces, you know, sugar cane fields, orange groves?" Alex kept swiveling her head back and forth to take in all the sights. There was a lot of traffic and stops, more than I remembered.

"That's further south. Up here, north and west of Orlando it's surprisingly built up. More than last time I came this way."

"What's with all the housing developments? What do you call them? Gated communities?"

"Some are gated. Depends. Different price ranges, from trailer parks to fancy high security compounds."

"And flags. Everyone seems to be flying American flags."

"You don't get that in England do you. No Union Jacks flying everywhere."

"Only on special occasions."

"So, in January, we get a lot of snowbirds. People from up North stay, like it and then retire here." Traffic was heavy as I stopped for another light. The trip was taking longer than expected. I leaned into the steering wheel and gazed at her. She caught me looking and sat up again adjusting her white shirt and checking her buttons. It was only a moment, but I think I expressed an interest in her she had not seen before.

"Snowbirds? Is that why there are so many eagles here? To eat the snowbirds? They have fancy names. Eagle Retreat. Eagles Nest. Eagles Last Resort. Do people get confused and go to the wrong one?"

I laughed.

"I thought they were cemeteries at first. But people live there?"

"Yes. Over fifty-five communities."

"Why aren't you in one?" She took off her sunglasses.

"Ouch." I gave her a questioning look. "In a cemetery?"

"No. One of these walled in communities."

"Have you seen where I live?"

"Yes. And its paradise. But you're only a few miles away from all this." She waved her hands around.

"Quite a few miles. So called civilization hasn't caught up with me yet."

"Will it?"

"Not in my lifetime."

"No wonder you want to retreat into your novels."

"It's not retreat." I frowned. Where was she going with this questioning? "And it's not Eagles Retreat."

"RV." She held her glasses in her hand and pointed at a large RV sign as we passed. "What do they mean? Is it code for something?"

"Recreational Vehicle. Like English caravans but bigger. We just passed a huge lot full of them. Some are like buses. But we're in America, so everything is bigger."

"Bigger roads. This would be a motorway in England. Two lanes each way?"

"We get into three lanes soon. More traffic too."

"America. That's another Walmart. And look another gun shop. Are there lots of guns here?"

"More than you can count." I shot her a knowing smile.

"How did you adapt to living here, coming from England?"

"I was just out of college. Miami wasn't so built up then as it is now, but it wasn't exactly peaceful. Here in central Florida, it's more relaxed. Everyone's armed and polite."

Alex frowned and kept absorbing the passing scenery, another car lot full of pickup trucks and RVs, further on a huge collection of identical golf carts, all new looking and waiting for buyers. Easy financing and no money down. She swiveled her head around.

"Golf carts? I've never seen so many. Is that a golf cart graveyard or are they new?"

I shrugged. "I'm sure the dealer gets the golf cart back when the owner dies, and he can resell it."

"Oh my. Look at that bridge! What is it for? A railway?"

"It's for golf carts." We drove under a large arched bridge.

"A golf cart bridge? The Villages? What is this?"

"The Villages? You've never heard of them?"

"No."

"That's why there are so many shopping centers along 27. The Villages are spread out over three counties and there are thousands of homes for the over fifty-fives there. And they drive golf carts. They have everything they need, doctors, clinics, town squares and lots of activities every night for all the residents. I was invited to an authors' reading night at a private home last year. I brought my novels and read the opening chapter of *The Dark Crimson Stones*. A great way to meet new people. Was I wrong."

"What happened?"

"Well, you've probably worked out I'm not very social, and I couldn't handle these aggressive women."

Alex guffawed and then held her hand over her mouth.

I took a deep breath and held my tongue. I've found women in their twenties and thirties at fantasy book conventions were more subtle and well-behaved than the older women in The Villages who were not interested in my books. I was talking to the wrong audience. I didn't see anyone bring one of my books for me to sign, and the sales were disappointing. I never returned. It's the sort of story you tell over a few drinks not while driving with someone you've just met.

"And they have a high rate of STDs there," I added.

"Making up for lost time." She sighed, still showing signs of amusement.

"Before they go to the cemetery," I added.

"Oh, reminds me of Evelyn Waugh. Do you like him?"

"I have all his books. Somewhere." I wasn't going to admit when I can't find a book, I know I have, somewhere, I order it again, only to discover the original copy hidden away on an obscure shelf. I did know where all my Waughs were. "*The Loved One*. Is that the title you're thinking of?

"Yes. How did you know?" She sat up straight and looked at me intently, although Evelyn Waugh would have hated my use of the adverb 'intently'. She put her sunglasses on again.

"Waugh would have a field day here, all the country clubs and golf courses and the ex-patriot English complaining about the crass Americans and their food." Alex waved her arms around.

"He'd write about a failed real estate salesman trying to sell homes in gated communities that are selling like crazy, but he couldn't sell one," I added.

"He'd have an older widow as a girlfriend, but he'd be an alcoholic and the ex-pats at his country club would be ashamed of him. Maybe he'd network in one of these churches and work for a funeral home on the side?" She pointed to another large church we passed.

I nodded. "There are quite a few aren't there? Churches I mean. Probably all packed on Sundays."

"You don't attend a church?"

"Do I look religious?"

"I don't know. Isn't it a good way to meet people?"

"Funny you should mention that because I tried once when I moved here."

"What happened?"

"I had nothing in common with them. I found the whole experience weird and never returned."

Alex continued to scan the ever-changing landscape.

"What's with these giant billboards? *One life can save the world*. What does that mean?"

I was wondering when she was going to comment on the billboards. I was seeing Florida through the eyes of a young Englishwoman who had not been exposed to the diversity—or was it the extremism?—of American culture.

"I don't think they're referring to Napoleon." Zach, the history teacher.

"Pro-lifers? Is that it?"

"Yes." I didn't want to say anything else based on what happened in my latest book. Alex would read about that soon enough.

"What made you invent new religions for your novels? Everyone seems to believe in either a shaman, like a witch doctor cult or a messianic leader who wants to seize power himself or replace an older established religion."

"I'm glad you understand the religious angle. I don't get much feedback about the beliefs of my characters. Consider the Middle Ages; Christianity was a huge deal in Europe. It was the basis for almost all human behavior. Faith, prayer, rewards, and punishments in the afterlife. It was a huge motivator. Faith is the glue that holds together the social contract."

She moved her dark glasses down her nose and looked at me.

"Zach, are you going to go all John Locke on me now? Feudalism isn't exactly what Locke had in mind."

"See those orange groves. They go for miles. Either oranges or sugar cane. And John Locke isn't in my books, is he? I have philosophers, wizards, shamans, priests, charlatans, the works, and I hope it's not easy to differentiate who are the good guys, the bad guys and the really bad guys."

"You categorize them?"

"Only when I'm being flippant. But seriously, in medieval times the church, the priest, the Sunday service, all the ritual, music, incense, the light coming through stained glass windows in the cathedral, everything helped to create a transcendent experience. Poor peasants went back to work on Monday with hope and maybe faith."

"But not charity."

"Yes. I mean no. Look how abused the poor are in my series."

"I like the peasant family in your novels, the Smythes, how they suffered through no fault of their own. I have a feeling there'll be vengeance in the new book I'm about to read."

"Is it obvious?" I asked. I slowed at another intersection as we cruised past Haines City. She read the road sign.

"A city? They call this a city? Where's the cathedral? We were talking about cathedrals."

"Wait till we get to Bok Tower. Did you bring a camera? Your phone?"

"No. Left my phone at your place."

I gave her a stern look.

"What? Am I being schooled? Was I supposed to have my phone with me?"

"Did I tell you that?"

"No. I wanted a break. Besides, I closed all my media accounts before I left. And I was banned from Twitter."

"What did you do?"

I could see she was hesitating, wondering how much she was going to tell me. There was obviously a lot she was holding back, but that was fine with me. I had known her, what? Twenty-four hours? I was having a pleasant conversation with a fan I was attracted to. I was not her therapist or guardian.

"I promise I won't put it in my next novel." I smiled.

"Zach, you don't have Twitter in your Dark Crimson world," she shot back.

"I don't have Twitter, but there is a sort of grapevine there. News can travel long distances, fast."

She turned to face me. I kept my eyes on the road. Traffic was now very heavy and with all the red lights we were not making good time.

"You honestly don't know what happened?"

"No."

"Didn't your webmaster tell you?"

"Tell me what?" My grin did not give me away.

She inhaled and then sighed before she began.

"Zach. There was this big controversy about Princess Alexandrina on Twitter. You didn't know about this?"

I assumed the way she said my name indicated her mood, but I couldn't read her moods. Was she exasperated? Disappointed? Teasing? Friendly? I was at a loss. "What controversy?"

"It was a big deal for a few weeks, up to the release of *Pilgrimage*. When I got banned from Twitter."

"What did you do?"

"Well, things were going wrong for me, and I took it out on a few online warriors who turned out to be wimps. I shouldn't've done it, but it felt good at the time."

"My heroine. I'm so proud of you, sticking up for me."

"Then you did know?"

"I'm not exactly a hermit sitting on top of a hill in my sack cloth, am I? Talking of hills, here we are."

I was saved from explaining how my webmaster had precipitated the entire 'Dark Crimson Twitter War' as it came to be known. We arrived at the large sign for Bok Tower Gardens and drove up the hill, past orange groves, a young pine forest and signs for walking trails before I came to the entrance, a small building where you could drive through the arch. I stopped to see a man in an official jacket try to lean into my Challenger.

Looking at Alex, he asked if I wanted to buy an annual family membership to save money. I turned to Alex who pulled a face, and I bought two single adult tickets and as the man gave me my change and tickets, Alex whined loud enough for him to hear.

"Daddy, you're always so cheap."

I smarted. The engine rumbled up the hill.

"What was with the daddy joke? And I'm not cheap."

"You don't go out much, do you?" She threw back.

I kept my mouth shut and parked under a tree in the crowded main parking lot. Mature oak trees covered in Spanish moss provided shade. Once I clicked the car lock there was an immediate silence followed by birdsong and insects. I took a deep breath and could smell dry pine needles.

"Do you want to take your jacket?"

"No. It's quite warm, isn't it? Is this normal for January?"

"It can get cold at night. What do you want to see first?"

"The tower of course."

"Christopher Robin." I grinned at her.

"What?"

"Your hat."

"Oh yes. Does that make you Tigger?"

"No, Pooh Bear. And not the Disney version, and I do like honey." She looked cute in her floppy white hat and dark glasses. I tried not to walk behind her. I wanted to look at the scenery without any distractions.

We bypassed the visitor center, the café and shop and headed up a path to the tower.

"I won't call you Pooh. Zach fits you perfectly."

I rubbed my stomach and smiled at her. A few sit ups and the bulge would disappear.

"You know A.A. Milne wrote an introduction to *Wind in the Willows*."

"Yes, sound advice. And I agree with him entirely." She adjusted her hat so she could see the tower over the trees ahead.

"You can smell camelias everywhere."

We heard the bells before the entire tower appeared from behind tall oak trees covered in Spanish moss.

"That's an amazing sound. Is that Bohemian Rhapsody?"

We walked around the tower to the large iron gate. The locked gate that led to the tower over a bridge was embellished with forged birds and snakes. I wondered aloud how they could get so much water up here. Then Alex asked about the coin machine.

"Food for the fish. Here." I slipped a quarter into the slot, turned the knob and got a handful of pellets that I gave to her.

Alex started to throw the pellets into the moat, and we watched the koi feed. We were like an ordinary couple in love, though we were not holding hands despite the looks we gave each other and the closeness of our bodies.

The structure itself glistened in the afternoon light; the Georgia marble appeared pink, and the intricate coquina stonework added to the drama of the structure.

"I've never seen anything like this either. Too bad we can't go in." We walked around the moat, until we came to the large golden sundial.

"Is that the Romeo and Juliet balcony?" Alex pointed out a red door and hand carved balcony above the vertical sundial.

"Maybe Rapunzel is at the top?" I turned to catch a glimpse of an enormous panorama of Central Florida from such a height and gasped. "Look at those rain bands in the distance. What a view."

"They're called vistas and Frederick Olmstead designed them, so you have a three hundred and sixty degree view of the peninsula."

"You're reading that." I pointed to the free booklet she held.

We continued along a path on the south side, stopping to take in the wide landscapes, the dramatic skyline with rays of sunshine spreading out from streaks of gray clouds. There were other people lying on the grass or on benches, but the entire garden was so well designed we were absorbed in our own green paradise.

"The light almost reminds me of a romantic painting. I can't put my finger on the painter."

"The landscape? The soft light? The sunsets here must be breathtaking, but Turner didn't paint orange groves." I pointed to the horizon. "You can see them further south."

We continued in silence as I kept looking first at the view, then at Alex, in this enchanted garden. "You have such a fair complexion, despite the sun and the mosquito bite, you have flawless skin. I wish I was a painter so I could capture you in this light."

"That's the nicest thing anyone has ever said to me. And coming from you it's not a pickup line."

"I can't imagine I've ever used a pickup line. Do any of my characters have pickup lines in my books?"

"No. They have ropes and chains. It's a different world." Then she put her hand to her face. "You can still see my bite?"

I felt too relaxed to make a smart remark. I shook my head.

We continued around the hill until we came to another path and a large pond full of water lilies surrounded by trees and shrubs on both sides. The tower appeared at the end of the vista, and I felt I had stepped into one of my books, in a magical sanctuary with Princess Alexandrina next to me.

Looking back, this was another opportunity where I could have held her in my arms and kissed her. There was a moment when we looked at each other but I walked away and came to a thicket of bamboo. I imagined you could squeeze inside but was loath to explore just as I was cautious about being too near my companion.

"The house is down there but it's closed." I looked at the signpost.

"I have to come up with another line instead of repeating what a great vista."

"There are so many."

I went to check my watch, an old habit I reverted to when stressed. My watch broke when I was building bookcases for my new home, and I never got it fixed. It was a gift from my school colleagues when I retired, and though I priced it at the time as being on sale for under a hundred bucks, I liked to wear it as a reminder of my high school history teaching days. It was a joke on their part because I was never on time at school. Now I took a quick peek at my smart phone. We had a seven o'clock reservation at Bern's. I didn't want to be late.

Alex led me through the visitor center, then the gift shop. She bought a couple of books as gifts and a collection of scented soaps. I carried her bag to the car.

"What did you think of the carillon?" I drove slowly down the road to the entrance, feeling relaxed from our short visit.

"Never seen one before and I loved the sound. I was expecting Disney, but I got old world Florida. Now I have more of an idea of what it was like here back then. Whenever back then was." She laughed. "Too bad we couldn't tour the old Spanish house. It looked authentic."

"You really need to spend all day here. Lots to see." I wondered if I should suggest another visit. What was I thinking? The day before I was filled with terror she might spend her entire vacation with me. I was getting used to having Alex next to me.

"I'm excited about the restaurant. I haven't been out on the town, you know, for some time. We'll stop somewhere to change?"

"Oh yes. Don't worry."

"And Zach." Her tone changed, as if I should pay special attention to her. I caught her eyes. "Don't take this the wrong way…"

"If you start with that phrase, I will take it the wrong way."

"Well, what I wanted to ask was." She paused again. "Why did you buy this car?"

"Seriously?"

"I'm just asking."

"It's simple. I got bored with my old reliable Honda. I don't have any toys other than a chainsaw and a few other tools. It's the fastest production car made in the US of A and my reward for all my writing. Does that satisfy your curiosity?"

"Yes. And I do love my seat."

I glanced over at her as she sunk into the leather. If this was a road movie I would pull over with screeching brakes, grab her in my arms and kiss her while pressing down on the accelerator in neutral to make all 8 cylinders roar. I tried to block out any more thoughts of Alex and my writing: towers, moats, giant water lilies and princesses with long hair and daggers hidden in their cleavage.

Alex had her sunglasses on again.

"The light here in Florida can be so bright."

"It's different from Thames Valley light, isn't it?" The setting sun was hitting our windshield and I lowered my sun visor.

"Is that why everyone here looks happy and fat?"

"We're not all fat. There were some good looking couples back there." I didn't want to think about the weight I was putting on. I was about to eat a large steak.

"I saw you ogling that blonde in tight pants. You even turned around to check out her bottom."

"It was a nice bottom." I mimicked how she pronounced bottom. "But not as good as yours."

"You noticed?"

"I'm a writer. I notice everything."

Alex kept quiet for the rest of the trip, moving her head, taking in the scenery, the gated housing communities, the giant SUVs and pickup trucks with political bumper stickers, the huge American flags flapping in the wind, as we approached Tampa.

.   .   .

We had stopped at a gas station to fill the thirsty Challenger. I changed into my navy blazer with matching shirt and red paisley tie. Alex walked out of the bathroom in a little black dress. All the men turned to stare at her. The dress emphasized her contours, her well-toned arms and legs.

"Is this it?" Alex turned her head as I eased under the portico of a large white building that could have been a warehouse with its low profile and no windows but for the sign by the entrance.

A valet parker ran to my car, and another opened Alex's door and was rewarded by the sight of Alex swinging her long legs out of the Challenger.

The lobby was a high ceilinged room illuminated with dozens of small lights and large gilt framed paintings. Everything seemed to be bathed in a burgundy glow. It was full of people waiting for their tables. We were seated immediately. I was not used to attracting so much attention, although no one was looking at me other than to figure out what had I done to snare such a beautiful young woman.

Our table was by the wall, in the center of the original dining room next to off-white bricks, a burgundy wallpaper and more gilt framed portraits. Our waitress presented us with large menus and a thick wine book.

Alex, after checking out the other diners and décor, asked, "Do they know you here?"

"I've dined here enough for them to remember me." I didn't want to explain I had given the owner's son a set of my books at a recent fantasy convention in Orlando and ever since I could call and get a last-minute reservation. I took all the eager producers who wanted to buy the rights to my books to Bern's. And of course, I made sure to always leave a memorable tip. It was the one restaurant where I could impress a visitor, no matter how jaded they were.

Over dinner we fell into a comfortable silence, like an old married couple. She would look at me and raise her eyebrows or smile, then moan as she ate. I wanted to concentrate on my steak and felt no need to engage in conversation. I was impressed Alex reacted in the same way and didn't bother me with questions about my books or where I lived.

Later, we were escorted upstairs to the Dessert Room, with its famous booths made of redwood wine casks, each with a retro sound system and an old fashioned telephone to call in your favorite song for the resident pianist to play. With the dim lighting and ornate antiques and paintings, our booth felt quiet and cozy. The pianist was on a break.

"How was your filet?" I asked.

"Perfect. You got the porterhouse?"

"Yes. I might have to walk home; I feel so full."

"I can drive, and you can run beside me," Alex offered.

Our knees almost touched under the table.

"How's your cake. How many layers? Twelve?"

"They should call it death by chocolate, and your crème brulée?"

I moaned and closed my eyes. I was imitating her, but she didn't get the joke.

The waiter came with our espressos. Alex asked for a brandy, but I convinced her to try a bourbon. A Texas bourbon. The waiter nodded his approval.

We sipped our espressos and kept exchanging glances, as if one of us was about to reveal a secret or start a difficult conversation. I was saved by the arrival of the Texas bourbon, delivered with flourish to Alex, who smiled and thanked the waiter, most likely making his night.

She brought her drink to her nose then took a sip, ran it around her mouth, held it for a moment as she stared at me, then slowly swallowed. It was a performance that enraptured me, as it was probably designed to, with her sensuous lips and bewitching eyes.

"How is it?" I asked.

"It's bold and spicy with a complex finish." She fixed me with a straight face then whispered. "Like your novels." She laughed.

I kept quiet. I didn't know how to reply.

"Zach." She paused, wanting my attention. "You drift away at times. I have no idea where you are or what's going on in that mind of yours." She made it sound like we had been together for a long time.

"I'm a writer. I'm always thinking about my work." Which was usually the case but not this evening with Alexandrina.

"Not your car? I can't believe you gave it to the valet. Did you see the expression on his face?"

"Don't worry, I gave him the valet key. He can't do much damage; besides, I have GPS hidden somewhere. Here." I took out my smart phone, opened my GPS car app and showed her where it was parked. Luckily for me it was stationary. "See where he put it?" I opened another app and showed her my dashboard camera. She saw my car was parked next to a Ferrari.

"Do you have a camera inside as well?"

"Oh no. And no audio either. I've been known to vent my frustrations on drivers by using creative language. Auto Tourette's syndrome."

She giggled. Was I really so funny? I was only recycling jokes she hadn't heard.

"I've never seen you use your phone, other than for this reservation. Don't you use it much?"

"You know, we could take some photos here if you like? Is that okay?" She nodded and swept her hair back, adjusting a curl that dangled over her face. I had no idea why I didn't take any photos at Bok Tower Gardens. Perhaps it had something to do with my ambivalent feelings towards Alex. I didn't want to give her any ideas but here I was feeding her at a famous restaurant and between us we had drunk enough to give me, what, courage?

The waiter hovered near our table as he saw I had opened my camera app. I handed him my phone. He took a couple of photos and returned it to me. I looked at them, thanked him then showed Alex.

"You look very happy," I said.

"So do you. Which reminds me, can I get a Wi-Fi password? I need to check my emails when I get back. You can AirDrop me the photos."

"Sure. Are you in a hurry to get back?"

She gave me a funny look. Did she have something planned or was she hoping I would make a move? I had no idea how this sudden relationship would develop. I was still thinking about the look she gave me when she squeezed the honey at breakfast. I shook my head and decided I would keep quiet after our burst of conversation. And what did she mean by AirDrop?

If I described this as a comfortable silence, I would kick myself.

Alex kicked me under the table, then used her eyes to direct me to the alcove opposite ours.

I frowned at her. She whispered some celebrity's name. I turned and looked. When I displayed my indifference, she backed off.

The waiter presented me with the bill, and I slipped him a credit card.

"Don't you read it?" she asked.

"No. Been here enough to know how they operate. It's not about the money, besides daddy is not cheap."

Alex let out a guffaw, no doubt fueled by all the alcohol I had given her.

I wasn't trying to impress her, but people who scrutinized every item and questioned everything with the waiter annoyed me.

When we went downstairs the maître d' insisted on taking us for a private behind-the-scenes tour. Alex was genuinely impressed: the giant fish tank, the stacks of aged meat, we even had a peak at what appeared to be an endless wine cellar full of narrow alleys stacked with bottles of all shapes and ages. I forgot the details. All I could do was admire Alex's long legs as she walked gracefully through the kitchen. The staff gawked at her and there were lots of smiles and nods to me. To them, I was the lucky rich bastard with a beautiful young girlfriend. For just a moment I thought I was the lucky rich bastard with a beautiful young girlfriend.

The trip home seemed shorter. When I have eaten too much, I tend to drive slower which was good, as we passed several highway patrol cars on I-75. Traffic was light, but for an endless procession of 18-wheelers. Alex stretched out in her seat and her little black dress rode up her thighs. She gave me her dreamy expression and thanked me several times for the meal, the drinks, and the entire evening. She threw out superlatives in her English accent. Her voice was mellow, as she enunciated her vowels with a seductive tone. I would've crashed my Challenger if I kept glancing at her.

I switched on the hi-beams when I turned off I-75 to light up the road and surrounding countryside on this moonless night. We had the road to ourselves. My Challenger had soft red illumination for the dashboard and the light made Alex's skin glow.

She had been asleep for some time when I pulled into my driveway. I stayed in my seat after I turned the engine off. In the silence, I kept the red interior lights on, so I could gaze at her long legs, porcelain complexion, and the way her chest moved as she breathed. I convinced myself I was doing this for my book, for research into the reborn Princess Alexandrina. But I had my doubts.

Dozens of moths strafed the hi beams and the trees looked like bearded ghosts. I imagined an owl watching me. A magic owl had appeared in my last novel.

When she opened her eyes, it took a moment before she realized where she was. I turned the headlights off and only a small shaft of light over my front door illuminated the ground. I opened her door. The light under her door came on. I assumed she was about to raise her arms for me to carry her inside. I stepped back, she swayed and caught herself before she looked at the sky. There were no clouds. Alex was mesmerized by the sight of stars covering the sky. We stood there for some time taking in the sight of the heavens.

"It's so beautiful." She managed to gaze upwards, and moved closer to me, a little unsteady on her feet. I should have held her around the waist, but I didn't want to mislead her as to my intentions.

"And that smell, camellias?"

"Yes, they're in bloom And the stars are always in bloom."

"Zach, are you a poet too?" she slurred.

I kept one eye on her so she wouldn't fall.

She raised her left arm, and I took her hand to guide her into the house and to her bedroom. I watched as she turned and flopped onto the bed, her legs flying in the air before landing on the floor and her shoes falling off. The last mystery of the evening was solved. She was wearing black underwear. Not that it mattered. I placed her bag in the room and shut the door. I wasn't going to kiss her goodnight or tuck her into bed or dress her in my pajamas.

I stayed awake for some time thinking about Alex, how she had come into my life and how I wasn't responding to her subtle and not so subtle cues. And the way she uttered my name. I fell asleep exhausted.

3

THE LONG STRANDS OF HAIR

When I appeared showered, shaved, and dressed the next morning, Alex was in the kitchen with fresh coffee she had brewed. I had checked her open bedroom door; her bags were packed, and her bed stripped.

"I hope you don't mind, but I found the coffee."

"Smells great."

"You have a lot of food and supplies here."

"I only shop once a month if I can help it, and I used to shop for an old couple up the road. The last time I dropped in on them was…" I trailed off and poured myself some coffee. She looked at me, no doubt sensing she shouldn't ask what happened, which was good because the old couple I had known since I had moved here had committed suicide. I tried to wipe the sadness from my face and sipped my coffee as she continued to look at me.

"I need to give you the Wi-Fi password. Here." I took an index card from a drawer and handed it to her. Her smartphone was next to her coffee cup.

She entered the password and raised her eyebrows as she started to scroll through an interminable number of emails. I sipped my coffee and watched her. She was dressed ready to travel, hair tied back, a black shirt and pants, and a handbag I hadn't seen before. Still no jewelry or make-up. She frowned and gritted her teeth, an expression I had not seen before.

"My ex wants me back. Says he made a mistake and wants to see me. Good riddance."

"You're not going to try again?"

"Are you kidding? It never works out."

"I wouldn't know."

She grunted. A new behavior. Would my Princess Alexandrina have grunted? She had snarled, many times, but never grunted. There was a difference. A snarl was a prelude or warning of an attack, a grunt was an expression of frustration.

"How much wine did I drink last night?"

"We only ordered one bottle."

"I must have had more than a few."

"Well, there was the aperitif, the Burgundy was so smooth, wasn't it? So many choices there, it's insane. Then you had a Texas bourbon upstairs or was it two? You seemed to like it. All in all, rather tasteful I thought. You can handle your liquor."

"I'm an Englishwoman in publishing. And you only sipped one glass."

"I was driving."

"I didn't make a fool of myself last night, did I?"

"Oh no. You were a sensation and a princess."

"I knew you'd say that."

I sensed she wanted to say a lot more but decided against it. She let out her breath through closed teeth, after a tense silence.

I sipped my coffee, stealing glances at her. She was still scrolling through her emails.

"Can you AirDrop the photos from last night please?"

I handed her my open phone. I heard a ping from her phone. She handed mine back and sighed as she looked at the two photos. She went back to checking her emails.

"Pierre is happy in Norfolk. Here." She thrust her phone at me to show a large black and white cat looking at me. I couldn't tell if he was happy or annoyed. She didn't mention her father. "There's disturbing news about a new virus from China. It's like the flu but supposed to be worse."

"Didn't they say that about bird flu and all the other scares we've had? I don't pay attention to such rumors."

"Too involved in your own world?"

I shrugged. I didn't have a polite way to reply. I should've paid more attention to this new virus, but I thought it would've been over in a few months. Just as my novels and the world I created have disasters that spread fear and panic with unpredictable consequences, I should've applied the same plotting principles, the same bizarre story logic, to my life and the coming pandemic.

"Anyway, I'm leaving shortly. I decided to see more of America while I can. Heading to New Orleans."

I put my lips together to form the word, oh, but no sound came out. I was getting used to her company, though I thought she was disappointed in me. Not the romantic lover she had hoped for who would sweep her off her feet. But she had only stayed two nights and I still hardly knew her. Though she did make a damn fine cup of coffee.

I ran to my study and retrieved a large Rand Atlas of the USA. "Take this. It's got all the major cities, and here." I opened it to show the route across Interstate 10 to New Orleans. "I-10 will take you straight there and beyond." When I pointed out the highway, I accidentally brushed her left breast. I withdrew quickly and felt embarrassed. I stole a glance at her, but she just fixed me with her eyes and then closed her eyelids for a moment. I had to admit she had a strong physical presence, and I naturally responded to this force, but I was fighting it as I was fighting my attraction to her. I felt I had to respond in some way but remained silent until I raised a finger. "Oh, I almost forgot."

I gathered a set of my novels from a box in my study. "What do you want me to say?" I had my magic marker ready.

"Love to Alexandrina." She frowned. "Thank you."

I wrote *To my Alexandrina, with love* and inscribed all five books and the sixth she had brought followed by four Xs.

I thought she was about to cry, but she shuddered, closed her eyes for a moment, and stood.

I walked her to her car and loaded her bags in the trunk. It was a lot colder today, but she didn't seem to notice. I shivered, and she formally shook my hand. I thought she would kiss me, at least on the cheek, but a handshake it was. I didn't know how to read her actions; a little severe, almost hostile. Did she feel hurt, or rejected? I wasn't acting. I was sad to see her go.

In the middle of the driveway, I watched her car until she disappeared. I remained there for some time, immobile, confused and, I admit, depressed. I forgot how cold I was. Then I turned and headed to my study. I had the first draft to work on and new insights into Princess Alexandrina.

It only occurred to me later when I was making dinner, I hadn't given her my phone number. I had two photos of her but no e-mail address or phone number. I only had a cell phone, and few people knew the number. I had blown what could have been an exciting relationship. I had dared not fantasize about what could have happened and now those fantasies were gone. I would put what I felt back into my writing. Then I remembered I had promised her tea under the magnolia tree. I always kept my promises.

I opened my phone and stared at the two photos. I used my fingers to enlarge her image. Was I going to obsess over her?

Returning to my routine, I rose early and had oatmeal and two cups of coffee. I reread what I had written the night before, made corrections, and started another chapter. I broke for lunch, a sandwich under the magnolia, where I felt melancholy, gazed at clouds and thought of Alex. What was she doing now? Had she found a younger man in New Orleans? Did I know any fantasy or adventure writers who lived in Louisiana she could visit unannounced? I had to admit I was jealous.

I worked till dinner time, made myself a couple of boiled eggs and toast, before returning to my study, and wrote until I was tired. I was beginning to understand there was a void in my life. I opened my phone and looked at her face again. I enlarged it, took a screenshot, and saved it.

I kept opening the photo of Alex and staring at it. By the second day, I was annoyed at my obsessive behavior and printed a full-sized copy of the image and placed it on my whiteboard next to Princess Alexandrina's name. Now I could turn around from my desk and gaze at her, smiling back at me. I took four small magnets and placed another black and white copy of her on the refrigerator.

The woman who cleaned my house and did my laundry looked amused by the sheets in the spare room, and the photo on the refrigerator, but she said nothing. She probably found a few long black hairs on the floor, because I did when I stood in the bathroom. I retrieved the strands, put them in a plastic bag with a label, and placed it in my desk drawer where I kept my fountain pens. I don't know why, but I wanted to keep the hair. Without her cell phone number or email address, I wondered how many Alexandrina's could there be in London? I recalled she lived in Chelsea.

I found a couple of English sites where I could input first Alexandrina's name and then Alexandra's, limiting the search to London, but there were too many results. I narrowed my investigation to North London. With Alex's last name Burroughs, there were still a lot of possibilities.

I recalled how she had quickly changed the conversation when we were sitting in my kitchen having our first cup of tea. Did she know more but didn't want to tell me? I was distracted by her mere presence, Alexandrina in the flesh, to question her family tree.

.   .   .

The only excitement all week occurred when I retrieved the plastic bag with her hair. I stared at the strands for a long time, then transferred them to a paper envelope where they would be better preserved. I placed the envelope in my drawer. I had something tangible to remember her by other than our two photos. I thought Alex would have commented on the absence of any personal photos in my house. When I moved here, I kept all the framed photos of my wife in a box and could not bear to display them.

I kept the drawer open, intrigued that I could be so emotional about a few strands of hair. Hair, I had neither touched nor run my hands through. I imagined Princess Alexandrina's long black hair and how fine it was. Then I noticed a green box. I had forgotten what it contained. When I opened it, I recognized the gold chain necklace with a small diamond I had given Angela, a long time ago. It was one of the few things I had kept of her jewelry. I took the necklace out and held the diamond. It sparkled and I thought about Alex. Then I remembered my Angela and how she had unclasped the necklace and handed it to me. She said one day I would find someone who would make me happy, and that this woman would be worthy of wearing the necklace. The scene could have been out of one of my books. It was her way of permitting me to love someone else even though she knew how withdrawn and miserable I would be alone, without her.

For two years I had watched her endure chemotherapy even though we knew there was little hope. I witnessed the love of my life shrivel to a hairless skeleton, a ghost of the woman I worshipped. When she left me, I cut myself off from the world and concentrated, some would say retreated, into my fantasy stories. I couldn't say her name. Any emotional life I still possessed, I poured into my writing, for none existed in my everyday life.

Then Alexandrina knocked on my door. I didn't recognize my fate. I was bound into a dark world peopled by characters I had created, and I was afraid to take a risk, a gamble, on being happy again, connected to another human being who might feel the same way about me.

That night I sat under the magnolia tree wrapped in a blanket and sipped a large glass of bourbon. The revelation I was seeking in my novel was instead, happening to me. I was in love and in pain. I could finally acknowledge the state I was in. I felt like a warrior in one of my stories: charging into battle with my sword held high, screaming with joy, for I was in the greatest moment of my life, and not afraid of death or defeat. I could fill my lungs with air and know I had lived my life to the fullest.

I returned to my study and typed for the rest of the night. I poured out all the passion and anxiety and loneliness and despair I had experienced since moving to this house, and I felt my head was about to explode with the frenzy of my writing.

If I could cry, now would be the time to leak tears of joy. That was the one criticism from Angela. I never cried. I was physically incapable.

4

THE LONGEST KISS HELLO

Lying in bed at dawn I thought of Alex and how I could will her to return to me. I needed to hold her and tell her I wanted her more than anything in the world. Instead of obsessing over Alex, I switched to the fictional princess. How could I surprise my readers and myself by making her more ruthless?

I saw Princess Alexandrina changing into a mature woman, her wrath and vengeance fueled by rejected love. I was unsure about her dagger. She couldn't kill off all her enemies, or lovers, could she? Despite the tragedy, she endured in the last novel. She needed to fall in love and establish stability in her kingdom. I felt I was making progress with my final book in the series. I set to work reading and editing what I had written earlier. I was on fire and there was a new energy and passion in my writing I had not seen before. The sense of loss poured through me and coursed through the veins of my characters.

At lunchtime I estimated Alex's flight home to the UK from Orlando, unless she changed it, would be the next day. If Alex was going to return, she had to appear on my doorstep this afternoon or tonight at the latest. To say I was nervous and on edge was an understatement. I kept running up to the mailbox, by the side of the road. I feared she might have mailed a letter or left a note for me and not dared to see me again.

The more optimistic side of me hoped she would appear before dusk. By early evening I was still hopeful as I prepared a pasta dinner for two: tortellini with marinara sauce, and a salad with fresh tomatoes from my greenhouse. I sipped a glass of red wine while I listened to Lester Young, loud enough in the front room for me to hear. Then I turned the music off because I didn't want to miss the sound of her car approaching. I couldn't eat. I was too agitated. I returned to my study and tried to write, with little success, nor could I reread what I had previously written. I couldn't concentrate.

Later, during a tea break, I checked her flight. It had to be tomorrow afternoon. I checked the clock on the microwave. It was past eleven. Unless she was dropping by on her way to the airport, I wouldn't see her.

I resisted the urge to run to my mailbox again.

I returned to my study and tried to read what I had written earlier and again I couldn't focus on the words.

I pushed my chair back from the desk and went to brush my teeth. After, I was going to sit on the porch, but I heard tires on the gravel. I rushed outside to see an unfamiliar car approach the house. The headlights blinded me. I stepped back into the doorway next to the umbrella stand and shielded my eyes. The lights went out and I saw her long legs swing out of the car.

"Am I glad to see you," she shouted as she ran towards me.

I stepped off the porch and held out my arms to welcome her, a big smile on my face. We came together, first a tentative hug, then a tight embrace. We drew back enough to kiss while our bodies were glued together. Our short kiss was followed by a longer one that merged into an even longer kiss. I have never been so spontaneous in my whole life. I felt recharged.

She eased away from me enough to ask if I was going to invite her inside. I grabbed her by the waist and pulled her into the house, down the hall, and into my bedroom. We didn't say a word.

We undressed, in a hurry. We held each other, naked. We were both shocked at our heated reaction once our bodies were pressed together. I took her face in my hands and kissed her, slowly, then ran my hands down her back to her tight bottom. She responded with force and wrapped her arms across my shoulders while her legs locked around my hips. I moved her to my bed, and we began to make love with a frenzy I would have found frightening under other circumstances. Alex put her honey-squeeze grip to work as we dealt with the tensions of our separation. We slowed down to gather our breath and concentrated on making each other climax for as long as we could manage.

Alex had me in a position I had never been in before and guided me inside her before she whispered in my ear, "You can squeeze them, they're real." She was looking down at me, enjoying my delight in her body. I needed no invitation as Alex continued to drain me of energy.

Later Alex laid across me. I felt her heartbeat against mine. Our breathing and heart rates came together as we slowed down, and I stroked her hair. We didn't need to talk. We kept kissing, tender kisses, and holding each other. This was, at last, what I would call a comfortable silence.

We woke in the middle of the night and started kissing again, our hands wandering over each other. I knew now what excited her and gave each body part just enough attention to make her scream for more. She had a way of reviving me and teasing me back that drove me crazy. She was extremely loud, and her moans and cries inspired me. I was glad I had no neighbors.

Later, at dawn, she whispered in my ear. "I had to return your map."

We giggled like two teenagers in love, which in a way we were. I felt very young and lightheaded. After gazing at each other's bodies and running our hands over each other, I started to kiss her lips and I couldn't stop. Thick, sensuous lips. I had completely underestimated how kissable her lips were. I had to correct Princess Alexandrina's lips but that could wait. And another mystery was solved about the real Alexandrina. I was not going to talk about it, but I have never described pubic hair in my books. Maybe I could introduce this in my last book, without it being a revelation? My characters did have sharp knives and razors. They used wax seals on letters.

"You've got a different car." I could be the master of the obvious.

"How observant of you. I broke down this morning somewhere in the Panhandle. I was racing to see you and it took me forever to get a new car. I didn't know if you would be here, and I didn't have your phone number."

"I didn't have yours either. I wanted to call you but couldn't."

"You know I hated you when I left."

"I thought something was wrong."

"Something? I was throwing myself at you and you were ignoring me. I was livid."

"You hid it well. I must confess, I was confused, unsure, whatever. I didn't understand."

"Me neither."

"Are you flying out tomorrow? I mean today?"

"Yes. I tried to change my flight but can't, and I'm due at work on Monday morning."

"Then we better make the most of our time." I ran my hands down her back and across her shoulders. I could feel her muscles, her body responding to me. I breathed in the scent of her hair, the smell of her sweat, like orange blossoms.

"I love the way you do that."

"You must do yoga; you're in such great shape."

"You can see how flexible I am."

"Oh yes." I was no longer thinking of the imaginary Princess Alexandrina. I was holding the real Alex in my arms and absorbing the warmth, the dampness of her body. "I missed you."

"Zach, the night I left you I cried myself to sleep in some motel in Alabama. It was so depressing."

I kissed her shoulders and ran my lips down to her chest before kissing her breasts and her nipples. Everything about her body captivated me. I had her wrapped in my arms. We held each other in silence for some time.

"I was determined to get to New Orleans. But when I got there all I could think about was how you would love what I saw and how good a traveling companion you were."

"You could've turned back."

"I asked myself that every night. I really missed you, but I fought it. And you weren't into me, were you? I didn't think you'd want me, yet I couldn't stop thinking about you." She wiggled; her legs wrapped around my body. I felt so complete, so at ease. "It took me forever to convince myself I had to see you again and if you would fly into my arms. I had no idea how you'd react. I couldn't bear another night retreating to the spare bedroom and you acting cold to me. That was my biggest fear. Being rejected by you."

"You had to confront your fear."

"Yes! It's like Princess Alexandrina being told by Prince Sammanke's father she had to face her biggest fear to be free and discover who she was."

"Oh." I was at a loss for words. I didn't want to tell her what would happen to the Prince. My writing was coming back to haunt me with the Princess's own words. I ran my hands up and down Alex's back and enjoyed her moans and the way her legs rubbed over mine. Glued together, we fell asleep.

.   .   .

We had time to eat the brunch I had prepared, under the magnolia tree. I wrote her physical address, her email address, and her phone number in a notebook with my Montblanc. There were small puffy clouds in the sky and the weather was unusually mild. She wore jeans and a white shirt, her hair in a ponytail.

"I saw you had my photo on your refrigerator."

"Yes. Your image is on my whiteboard as well. Helps me write."

"I meant to ask you why you write with a fountain pen."

I saw her looking at the large pen. I screwed the cap on and smiled.

"Better the smell of fountain pen ink than blood."

Alex ran her hands through her hair as she thought about this.

"I've never read that in your books. I would've remembered."

"In *Pilgrimage*, Princess Alexandrina has a new writing instrument. I describe the smell of the ink she uses. You'll have to read it to find out the ingredients."

"On the plane. Oh!" She leaped out of her chair. "I almost forgot." She ran inside and returned with a gift basket. "It's for you. I know you love coffee and baking from all the baking pans you have."

I took out a can of Café Du Monde and a package of Beignet Mix.

"That's wonderful, you checked out my kitchen before. Too bad we don't have enough time for me to make beignets. I love them freshly dusted in sugar. I'll cook you something special, next time."

"I hope that's soon." She sighed and if I was not mistaken squirmed in her seat. "My father has the same big pen. It feels odd seeing you with it. A gold nib. It's the 149, right?" She smiled and pushed the hair from her face.

I nodded and poured her more tea from the white teapot. I had no idea how to reply to her observation. Should I ask her about fountain pens or question her about daddy issues? She had called me daddy at Bok Gardens, and it was too late to ask about it now. We sipped tea and looked at the magnolia tree, the clouds, and each other. A red cardinal appeared on a branch above us. In my books, there was a special all-red bird, the dark crimson bird of love, that appeared when two people were in love. She saw the bird first and glanced at me. We exchanged smiles but did not speak.

I got up and ran into the house. I returned with a green box.

"I want you to have this. I noticed you don't wear jewelry, but I hope you like it."

She opened the box and gasped. I was waiting for tears, but she methodically threw back her hair, secured the necklace, and adjusted the diamond. It fell perfectly on her white shirt.

"It's beautiful. Thank you. It's old, right?"

"Yes. I wanted you to have it." I resisted the urge to unbutton her shirt and kiss her. "Why don't you wear jewelry? You don't even have earrings, but your ears are pierced."

"My last boyfriend bought me a lot. When we broke up, I returned everything to him. But now I have this. Thank you." She rose from her seat and kissed me. I wanted the kiss to last forever. She tasted like honey. Then she broke away and looked alarmed.

"What?" I asked.

"I haven't taken one photo this entire trip."

"Oh. Didn't you take any in New Orleans?"

"No. I was too upset. And I don't do selfies. Until now."

Alex took out her cell phone. She knelt by my chair and took several photos of us.

"Here, I want to take some photos of you. By the tree." I offered and took her phone.

She posed and we swapped places. I now had some photos of Alex that I would never have thought of taking on my own.

"Can I get some pictures of your house? And garden? I want to remember everything."

"Go ahead." I followed her around the garden, and she shot a few images of the back of the house. She asked about the inside. I nodded. I just didn't want her to take any photos in my study. There were too many secrets about the next book in there. My kitchen and the front room got covered, then the front room with the red crates of vinyl records and my sound equipment. Alex was on her knees trying to include all my *Wind in the Willows* editions. I could now feast on how delicious she looked in her shirt. She took the last ones of me next to the Challenger. I had her AirDrop photos to me, now that I knew what AirDrop was.

I helped Alex load her luggage, and she followed me to her car rental return near the airport. I waited for her while she got her receipt then drove her to her terminal to park in a short-term lot.

At the ticket counter, Alex had to check her bags. One was overweight. Full of my books. The woman behind the counter with short green hair looked at Alex and told her she could rearrange her bags or pay the extra fee. I stepped in.

"I'll pay. It's no problem. They're my books." I smiled back at Alex and then at the woman with green hair. She took my credit card and read my name.

"You're Zacharias Hideman." She gasped.

"Yes." Thinking she was checking it was a real card.

"Oh my god. I stood in line and bought your latest book. *The Dark Crimson Pilgrimage*. I'm a big fan." She handed me my card.

"Oh look, the weight's gone down again. You're all set. Alexandrina Burroughs." She read the name again on the boarding pass and a light went off. "Of course. You're the Princess. Wow!" She handed the pass to Alex who allowed herself a close-lipped smile.

"Thank you, Kelsie." I had leaned over to read her last name. "See you at the next book launch."

"Can't wait." She exclaimed as Alex and I walked towards security.

We had one last goodbye kiss before the security line and we agreed to write to each other, letters, real handwritten letters as well as phone calls and video calls. I insisted on letters I could read and reread. I promised to plan a trip to England and spend time with her once I had completed a reasonable draft, and of course, she was dying to read it.

Before I got distracted on the drive back from the airport, I called my webmaster. He was surprised to hear from me as I usually emailed him instructions or questions. I had not physically seen him for some time. I had no idea what other jobs he did apart from working for me and didn't want to ask him. I told him to look up a Kelsie in our database and ship her a Princess T-shirt with a thank you from me. Kelsie with an ie. I spelled her last name for him as well. He was hopeless at spelling. I had to carefully proof everything he uploaded onto my website. We talked about how readers were responding to *The Dark Crimson Pilgrimage* on social media and the sales of the new merchandise going through the roof.

On the way home, I ran through all the scenes in my head; from Alex knocking on my door up to when I kissed her goodbye at the airport. I was elated; I had a girlfriend who was thirty years younger than me. I was sad because she had flown away. There were only two other times in my life these powerful and confusing emotions had coursed through my body. In a sense, I felt like an eighteen-year-old again, when I first met Alexandra until the day her brother caught us in the act. But there was something in the back of my mind that felt odd, something I did not understand.

5

LOVE LETTERS IN THE MAIL

I was highly motivated to finish my book. My girlfriend was in London, over 4,000 miles away. I could finally tie up all the loose storylines and resolve my characters' fate, once and for all. The only distraction I had were all the photos. I could not stop looking at her. The one from Bern's, on my whiteboard and refrigerator, was still my favorite.

Her comment about her father and the fountain pen got me thinking. We never did discuss our age difference. I could be the same age or older than her father. But my connection with Alex felt natural. I was at ease with who I was and my age. I thought she was mature. The difference didn't matter. I found her youth and energy inspiring. I cuddled the pillow we had used in our lovemaking. It gave off her scent, and I could not get enough of her. I fell asleep dreaming of my Alexandrina.

Alex called me the next afternoon, from her flat in Chelsea. She told me to download a free app so I could video phone for free. We scheduled another call later and talked for an hour. She lived alone. She was naked, and she missed me, probably as much or more than I missed her. I've never had a long-distance relationship, but video calls were fast becoming my favorite way of communicating, although I would blush if I had to recount what we said or displayed to each other. I was expecting her to tease me about Kelsie at the airport, but she must have forgotten about her, which was good, so I assumed Alex did not feel insecure that I would run off with a younger woman with green hair.

Alex had finished my book on the plane. "It was uncanny reading about Alexandrina after being with you. I felt an even stronger connection to her as if we were related. It was weird. But I loved the book. It's the best one yet. So often in a series, the storyline runs out or it gets old, but *Pilgrimage* was so exciting. I'm going to read it again, just to wallow in the words. Now I know about the blood in the ink. And Princess Alexandrina." She sighed. "It's a little sick, isn't it? Using the blood of the baby from her miscarriage? It was a miscarriage, wasn't it? Or was it an abortion?"

"You're going to have to read the final one to know for sure."

"I hate the way you do that. You have all these twisting plots going from one book to the next."

"That's why it's a series."

We stared at each other on our screens. Alex looked like she was waiting for more.

"You know smells are important in my stories. Did I tell you I haven't wash my sheets? I love your smell, your body scent. You know you have two, one from your body, your arms and shoulders and hair, and the other one down there. It drives me crazy."

"I feel the same way about you but coming back to the Princess. She was angry, wasn't she? And at the end, she blamed Prince Sammanke for her miscarriage or abortion? Does that mean he's the next to go? And isn't he her cousin? They don't know that do they?"

"Oh, you are way ahead of me. You'll have to wait till you read what happens to Alexandrina and Sammanke. I can't tell you now, you'll just have to read it."

"I can't wait. You'll send me a draft, won't you? As soon as you've finished?"

"I promised and I promise. But you might be surprised."

"No. Don't do that to me. She isn't killed, is she?"

"Oh no. And I'm not saying any more. Because I have no idea myself."

"You're hiding something from me, aren't you?"

She had known me for such a short time and already knew me better than I knew myself.

"You'll find out soon, I hope."

"Oh, the suspense is killing me."

.   .   .

I handwrote a letter the next day and airmailed it from my distant but local post office. I had a supply of heavy crème paper and matching envelopes. Despite all the time daydreaming about Alex and writing and rewriting letters and the long video calls each night, I managed to make progress with my first draft. As I told Alex on one of our calls, *The Dark Crimson* world wasn't superficial; there was no consumerism, no media influencers, no fluff if I could use such a modern term. Everything was life or death, blood and guts, spiritual and mud caked. Characters were driven by shamans, religious zealots, witches and wizards, and a strict feudal order where peasants meant nothing to the rich, the powerful, and the ruling class. Until, and I did not tell Alex this, Princess Alexandrina has a revelation and sides with a new spiritual leader who doesn't condone violence as a means to maintain power.

.   .   .

In our next video call, Alex wanted to talk about social media.

"You've got a big social media presence. Your fans post photos of themselves dressed up as your characters, in your T-shirts, holding your books, quoting passages. I could go on and on. I know your webmaster does his job but why don't you post your own material? You could generate more fans for your email list, couldn't you?"

"I don't look at anything online. I'm too busy writing."

"I'm surprised you're not on Twitter, practically every writer and editor are on that platform, it's how they keep in touch and share information, and bitch to each other."

"Never used it," I replied. "And look what happened to you. You're banned from Twitter."

"That's not the point and I did that because I was sticking up for you before I knew you." I could see her frowning at me. "But you're a loner, aren't you? Stuck in the middle of nowhere and surrounded by alligators."

"Are you still upset about me stopping you from taking off your clothes to swim with alligators?"

"Yes." She pouted, then laughed. "We'll always have that story."

I couldn't help but laugh with her. Watching her face light up on my laptop was a delight.

"I remember how you kept looking at the water as if a giant alligator was going to appear and snatch you in its jaws."

"That's what you led me to believe."

"The power of words."

"You just didn't want me taking off my clothes. I would have seduced you."

I watched her strip, first her sweater then her shirt, bra, trousers, and panties, until she stood naked before me. She looked defiantly beautiful.

"I admit I didn't know what I was missing, but I do now, and I do so miss you. It's not fair doing that to me." I looked at her in silence as she slowly turned around and lowered her eyelids for a moment then gazed at me. They were gray blue in color and appeared to brighten in the light she had directed on her face.

"You've woken something in me I didn't know I still had."

"You're not coming up with a dragon reference, are you?" she teased. I could see her chest now, close up.

"You know I have no dragons in my books."

"Only Hounds of Truth." She kept swaying back and forth.

"Exactly. What were we talking about?" I couldn't concentrate, mesmerized by what I saw on my screen.

"Something about me awakening something in you, that sort of thing."

She was enjoying herself and I couldn't keep my eyes off her.

"Do you know what I miss about you the most?"

Her face came into focus as she raised her eyebrows and pursed her lips.

"Kissing you. When I'm kissing you, I feel we're having a separate conversation with our lips."

"And tongues," she added, opening her mouth and licking her lips. "Don't forget the tongue."

"It's on a sublime level. Your tongue can be very assertive."

"Is that a bad thing?" Her facial expression looked exaggerated on my laptop.

"No. It's almost too much and I'm on sensory overload."

"I can't wait to kiss you again."

"Yes, all this teasing is driving me crazy."

Her chest occupied my screen again. Her areolae were a bright red, and her nipples were erect.

"Well, you succeeded in turning me on," I admitted. "But now you're too far away."

"You could come over. Even for a long weekend?"

"That's a thought. Let's see how my writing progresses."

"Can I inspire you?"

.   .   .

A few days later I received a poem in iridescent purple ink.

33 1/3 IS FAST ENOUGH

You keep your original jazz albums
in wooden fruit crates
the needle on the turntable costs more
than a diamond tiara
speakers are the size of coffins
and the fireplace improvises loud sparks
33 1/3 is fast enough

I was impressed. All I needed was for her to be lying next to me on the red sofa. And no, the color was not deep crimson.

I sent her a poem.

GLUE

Being glued to you
On the damp sheets
I don't think I am allowed
So much happiness
I'll just take what I can get now
And not care about tomorrow

Like the characters in my novels
Something bad always happens

I don't think I can stand so much happiness
It makes me very nervous.

Alex thought I was cheating myself and should accept what we had together. Allow yourself to be happy, she wrote. Our lives were not like the characters in my books. She wrote another poem in deep blue ink.

That first night I came into your room
I could not help myself
I had to see you
I stood over you for some time
I watched you dreaming
And imagined you were dreaming of me.

I read the poem for the umpteenth time and thought what a contrast from when I met her. If I had awoken that first night and seen her looking at me, I would have been terrified and thrown her out, but now I am entranced by the image of her gazing at my dreaming self. What does that say about me?

·   ·   ·

On another video call, Alex read me a poem. She promised it would arrive in the mail, but she wanted to read it to me. She was wearing a sheer teddy and I thought this was sheer torture as she said it was about the time we went to the steakhouse, and I got her drunk.

"You told me you could handle your drink."

"Look how much you gave me. When you took me into your house, I was a little intoxicated, but I knew what was going on."

I grunted.

She held a piece of paper to read, hiding her chest.

I wanted to kiss you with a billion stars as witnesses
I wanted to kiss you with a family of raccoons spying
    on us
I wanted to be kissed by you with no moon to see us
I wanted to be kissed by you in darkness
but you led me into the guest room
and watched me fall into bed
with my legs up in the air
so you could see my thong.

I wanted to be kissed by you naked
I passed out in my little black dress

Alex could see how I was smiling.

"I never told you about the raccoons."

"Don't underestimate my powers of observation." She lowered the poem, and I had a close-up view of her. "And I saw you lurking in the doorway. I gave you a little show and you still didn't react."

"It didn't seem the right thing to do. And you were drunk."

Looking back, I thought we needed the physical separation of a few days to work out our feelings for each other. If we had slept together that night our relationship would not have been so deep. She was drunk. I was afraid to start anything with a woman thirty years my junior. A writer's imagination can be a curse or a blessing.

"Do you like the teddy or the poem?"

"I love both and I can't wait to hold your poem. I can't wait to hold you."

"Thank you for the gift card. I wanted to show you what you're missing."

"I'm so torn. I want to jump on a plane now and see you, but I need to finish my draft. If I came over, I might not want to leave."

"Could you live in London again?"

"After living in this paradise? And this heat and sunshine? I don't know. Our winters here are quite mild compared to yours."

"Yes. I know. It didn't feel cold. Not like London cold."

"I couldn't survive a winter in England. You can always come here again. You know that. Just tell me when you're arriving. I'll pick you up."

"It's tempting. So tempting. But let's see what happens. You should finish your manuscript first. We all have priorities. It's one of the annoying things about being an adult."

"Being an adult sucks!" I made a pouty face and she laughed. It was the first time we had seriously discussed our future. Who would live where and how? All unanswered questions but at least we had options. My dear departed wife's favorite word, options.

.   .   .

Later that night I wrote a letter I never sent Alex. I had alluded to Hallmark movies my wife liked to watch even though they were predictable and romantic in a sanitized middle-class fashion. The ending was always safe and happy. Two unexpected lovers finally realized they were in love with each other, kissed chastely, and got married. The story I imagined for Alex and me was where the dark side of R.H. Hyde took over; everything went wrong, terribly wrong. At the time I had no idea how wrong, but I was glad I never sent the letter.

I knew Princess Alexandrina was different from the real Alexandrina. Though if she read the latest draft, she would see they were becoming closer. I left that observation for later. One of the problems with living with a writer was you lived with your life intersecting with the writer's. My wife used to say things like, "You didn't put that in did you? How embarrassing. What will people think?" To which I would reply, no one will know you said it first.

6

NEWS FROM LONDON

My new routine of emails, video calls, and handwritten love letters lasted for six weeks before I received a strange email from Alex. I video-called her earlier than usual, anxious as to the mystery.

"Zach. I'm pregnant. I've taken two tests and went to the doctor this morning because I was feeling sick." She looked tired.

"Oh." I was at a loss for words. "How do you feel now?" I didn't want to congratulate her if she wanted an abortion. My first thoughts were elation, followed by terror.

"I'm in shock. It's yours, obviously, but we were only together one night."

"Yes, but what a night," I said. Male pride surged through me. I had made a baby. A little late in life but it was never too late. "It's a baby of love," I added.

She giggled then became serious. "I stopped taking the pill when I dumped my boyfriend. I never expected this to happen. What do we do?"

I frowned. One thing about video calls is you can convey a whole range of emotions with your face. I must have appeared awkward and confused. I had led a very orderly life before Alex knocked on my door.

I was going to be a father – if she kept the baby. My wife couldn't have children. Now I was offered this gift of life.

I did some calculations. Baby would be starting college when I was in my late seventies. I hoped the royalties would still be pouring in. At the back of my mind, I did want to start another series. It would pay for college.

The previous day I had received a detailed email from a new film producer who had read my *Dark Crimson* books and was serious about buying the rights. I replied immediately and suggested we set up a phone call. He was in Europe finishing another deal and would contact me in a day or so. I debated with myself if I should find a new entertainment attorney to negotiate the rights but thought it best to see what this new producer would offer. I didn't want to tell Alexandrina about this development until I had something solid to report. I had to get my head back into the baby situation.

"Whatever you do I'll support you. If you want to have the baby, then we can talk about what we can do. We have lots of options and we're both smart. If you don't want the baby, well…" I hated abortion in principle, but I didn't want to bring an unwanted baby into the world. I thought the mother should have the final say. She was the one carrying it. "We need not decide right away. You said you were in shock. Let's wait a few. No pressure. It's about what you want. I'll support whatever you want to do. And at the moment I have no idea what I want to do." I stared at her face on my screen. She looked dazed. "You could come and live with me here. I'll even let you drive my Challenger." She gave a little smile. "You could work from here, doing editing, proofreading, editing stuff, remotely. Occasionally fly somewhere to do business. But you'll find people want to come to Orlando anyway. You won't be cut off or isolated."

"Zack, do you want me to keep it?"

"My initial response is yes. But I'm in shock as well. Let's give ourselves some time to think this through. We have time and resources."

"You know I made a promise to my aunt I would raise a Jewish child."

"Yes, you told me. I understand. You should honor your aunt and mother."

"Then there's this other complication. The virus from China everyone's calling COVID-19."

"Oh." I must have looked like an idiot. I knew there was a flu epidemic and some other virus that was deadlier but isn't there always one in winter? Tucked away in the middle of Florida and not following the news, I had no idea what was happening.

"There's speculation that countries are going to shut down flights and close borders, to stop the spread of the virus. It's extremely contagious and the authorities are getting worried." Alexandrina looked anxious.

We talked for a few more minutes, but she was exhausted, and I didn't want to ask more questions about the virus affecting our plans. We hung up.

I walked around the house muttering about what had happened. I pictured a dark character from my books lecturing me. Being with Alex felt so right but what if I was fooled? "What if she had an affair with a younger man in New Orleans? They could've been doing it all week and he would've gotten her pregnant. Only he ain't such a catch, is he? A shady character, with no money, and no prospects. How do you know this didn't happen?"

I had lived alone for years, had few close friends, and no close female friends. Most of the women I knew were my wife's friends and they abandoned me after my wife died, through no fault of mine other than I moved from Miami. Well, there was one of my wife's girlfriends who kept in touch, even came to visit me here but she gave up. I wasn't interested in her romantically. I couldn't imagine going to see my silver-haired poet friend up the road and telling her, oh, by the way, I got a woman thirty years my junior pregnant after just meeting her. What do you think I should do? I couldn't see that conversation going well.

I went back to my laptop and researched COVID-19. No wonder I never followed the news. A global pandemic was spreading rapidly, and no one seemed to know what to do. There were so many contradictory statements and opinions from scientists, doctors, and politicians. Reading the news always gave me the impression the sky was about to fall on my head.

.   .   .

Alex didn't call for two nights. I wrote her an email and another letter, expressing my love and support for her. I checked out her email address and found another one almost identical, related to her publishing house. I scanned the website but didn't see her name or her photo. I called the number and asked for Alexandrina Burroughs. She wasn't available. Did I want to leave a message? I hung up.

Not wishing to rouse her suspicions when we next talked, I asked for her work number in case I had to call her in an emergency. And her business email. We talked about her working from my home, freelance, with the baby in the spare room, to be renamed the nursery. There was no mention of an abortion, and I didn't want to bring up the subject. But our relationship had changed, from being carefree lovers for one night to concerned future parents separated by an ocean and the threat of a global pandemic.

I had to remind myself of the great revelation I had earlier, before she arrived from New Orleans, and how I felt so positive and passionate about her and what she meant to me.

7

I used the same app Alex had me download to meet with my new film producer, who had emailed me again from London. He had plans for turning the first book into an entire season of episodes. He was overseeing the final edit of a new film and had decided not to start the historical drama series he had considered. He wanted to switch to my *Dark Crimson* novels. He looked enthusiastic on screen and stated there was ample financing available despite the threat of lockdowns and canceled flights. We didn't talk specific numbers, but he was anxious to fly back to the States in his jet, secure the rights and start pre-production. I told him I had a girlfriend in London who wanted to fly over to see me and needed either a work visa or some other visa so she could stay. He told me about a fiancé visa and informed me of an immigration attorney he used in the US who handled all his crew's applications to work here. And when I told him her name, I made him promise not to hire her for the series, even if she looked like the real Alexandrina of the *Dark Crimson* world. He laughed. Talking about Alex cemented our relationship. I was not just a writer trying to sell an option.

I searched the internet and IMDB to check my producer. Everything he had told me looked true. He was well respected in the industry and presented his case well to me. I started to get excited.

With regard to my other relationship, I recalled my first impression of Alex and how I had resisted my feelings for her. I knew of no connection between my first love Alexandra and Alex other than they both grew up in North London. Checking Alex's hair in a DNA database could lead to other names linked to her. It was the only way I could think of relieving my apprehension, and I knew a private investigator in London who could help me.

I located a DNA testing site in Orlando. I took the envelope with her hair to the lab and deposited Alex's hair strands, with their follicles intact, into a small cardboard box. On my initial phone call, I discovered the receptionist/technician was a fan of my novels, and I left a signed copy of *The Dark Crimson Pilgrimage* dedicated to her. I paid the fee, and she promised the results would be rushed to me by email.

.   .   .

Alex's work phone number checked out to where she was employed. Her business email worked and matched the company's website. My suspicions were allayed, yet there was still a nagging doubt in the back of my skull. As a fantasy writer, the storyline always went wrong. Nothing works out as planned. I ask myself, what is the most horrible thing I can do to my characters? Then I make it even worse. Tension builds, my favorite characters are under extreme threat, the plot becomes more compelling, the reader is engrossed. The story advances.

.   .   .

Two weeks later I received the results by email. DNA didn't feature in my novels. I'm no expert in DNA, but I knew Peter T. Barnes, a private investigator. I had met him during a book fair in Chicago and spent an evening with him, talking about publishing. He wanted to write a book about his adventures in the P.I. world, and I told him what I knew over a few drinks. I dropped him an email and he replied immediately. Yes, he could help and had contacts with DNA labs and genealogy sites in the UK. I asked the price, and he said all I had to do was read the manuscript he had almost finished. I would've much preferred a cash transaction and told him to bill me for any costs he incurred, but he informed me, by return email, to send him all I had. I demanded a confidentiality agreement with him which he complied with.

I emailed the DNA results of Alexandrina Burroughs and the name of my first girlfriend, Alexandra, from North London, as if that would help, to Peter T. Barnes, P.I.

I had stopped working on my manuscript. The suspense was eating away at my insides. I still had to convince Alex we should ensure the baby was genetically healthy. We could do the tests a few more weeks into her pregnancy.

I arranged for a private pediatrician in Chelsea to accept Alex as a patient as I didn't trust their National Health Service. NHS was beginning to be overwhelmed with patients contracting the new virus, and I didn't want Alex to be exposed. We still talked two or three times a week for a few minutes and longer on weekends. I had a reserve of correct postage stamps so I could leave my letters in the milk can at the edge of my property, without driving to the Post Office.

At the same time, I heard airline travel was about to be shut down between Europe and the US, I received a large e-mail file from Peter T. Barnes, P.I. I opened the document, a full report under his P.I. banner.

The expectant mother of my child had a family tree linked through other DNA tests her family members had taken, including her aunt. I scanned through the report and looked at the sources he had used, birth records, genealogy websites, and other databases I had never heard of.

Alexandrina Burroughs was the daughter of Anne Beatrice Burroughs, who had died two years ago. Anne was the daughter of Alexandra Beatrice Burroughs, who had passed eleven years ago. Alexandra had been born in 1960 in North London. Alexandra had a brother Thomas Brian Burroughs who was two years younger and died when he was twenty. Peter T. Barnes, P.I. had included photographs, I presume from family albums, of the three women and the young Thomas.

The grandmother, Alexandra, had never married, and the father of Anne was not listed on the birth certificate. I recognized Alexandra immediately from the photos in the family tree. Anne had been born approximately nine months after we had broken up. Perhaps Alexandrina had never known Thomas, for she never mentioned him to me. I would have to ask her about him.

I printed the full report, including a blown up photo of the young Alexandra. Then I sat under the magnolia tree. I had enough light to pore over the names, dates, and photos in the late afternoon sun.

.　　　　　.　　　　　.

I could jump on a plane tomorrow and fly to London to be with Alex or I could arrange for a private plane to bring her to Orlando airport. I had a contact in a charter jet company and could afford for her to come over now before everything shut down. Or she could hitch a ride with my potential new producer.

First, I had to break the news to Alex.

The mother of my child was my granddaughter.

I was in love with my granddaughter.

I sat motionless for a long time.

An owl flew close by and landed on a branch. The owl stared at me, and I was reminded of a scene from my last book where Prince Sammanke had a silent conversation with his magic owl about Princess Alexandrina.

The owl blinked, and I realized I had three choices. The first we had already decided. Neither of us wanted an abortion. We could live as husband and wife, but I was uncomfortable about that arrangement, or we could live as grandfather and granddaughter, with our secret connection. I could convert my front room to her bedroom or the nursery. We would have to talk about the DNA results and what Alex wanted, once she knew.

I lifted my head to the darkening sky. The thin clouds on the horizon changed to a deeper pink and purple.

I didn't know if the tears streaming down my face were of sorrow or happiness.

THE ANONYMOUS BOTTLE
of CHAMPAGNE

A POST-PANDEMIC LOVE STORY

If I had a bucket list, I would have at the top, the act of sending the most expensive bottle of champagne to a beautiful stranger.

.   .   .

For the past week, I had stayed at a luxury hotel in Montreux and had grown comfortable dining in the main restaurant. The cold wind blowing off the lake made a night out too hard for my Florida constitution despite the promise of spring during the day.

I first saw her high heels as she swayed past my table. I detected a faint trace of her perfume. Dressed in an elegant black pantsuit, her brocaded jacket was designed to minimize her large chest. She was used to making a dramatic entrance as she swung her ponytail and scanned the half-filled room. She failed to notice me as she waltzed past. The waiter pulled out her chair by the window, and when I next peeked, she was gazing at the lake and snow-covered mountains.

At my usual spot, in a corner and suitable for a lone diner, I could observe everyone. As a private investigator, I don't attract attention. I'm of average height and average build, though I seem to be expanding in the middle. My hair is receding, so I keep it short and combed forward. I'm proud of my full mustache, but when people try to recall me, they always fail to describe it.

I was relieved few people were wearing face masks, indicating they were sick of the entire pandemic or didn't believe in them. I could now show my mustache.

I had another week at the hotel, a gift from my biggest client. He claimed it was a bonus for all the work I'd done for him during the pandemic. The hotel had awarded him the suite based on all the business he brought them. No complaints from me. Waiting for me in the suite was a luxury watch in an elaborate box with a welcoming note from my client. I had no plans to take the watch off my wrist and noticed the hotel staff paid more attention to me once they spotted the bracelet and distinctive bezel.

I hadn't traveled overseas in two years and had been dreaming about an indulgent vacation, and with my new watch, I was reminded of my champagne fantasy.

I called my waiter and confirmed the woman was dining alone. She had ordered a martini but was considering a local white wine to go with her salad. I had him summon the sommelier. I'm usually intimidated by sommeliers with their superior knowledge and attitude, but this young man was very charming. He placed the giant leather-bound book before me, open at the champagnes. Based on his recommendation we agreed on the vintage to be sent to her table. I emphasized I didn't want to be identified and naturally, I would compensate him for his discretion. My regular waiter listened and nodded his approval. He knew I was a generous tipper.

The sommelier marched out with the bottle and presented it to her. The waiter followed with the silver ice bucket and stand. Diners watched as the sommelier made a show of unsealing the foil, loosening the cork then managing the load pop before carefully pouring the golden liquid into a long fluted glass. An older American couple seated nearby was mesmerized. I pretended to be indifferent as I read my book and nibbled on some cheese, though I didn't miss the spectacle out of the corner of my eye.

She scanned the room again, and I saw her whisper into the sommelier's ear and place something in his hand.

Once I had finished my espresso, I called for the check, signed it, and left a cash tip for the waiter. With studied indifference I walked to the elevators, not daring to look back, knowing I had fulfilled my fantasy. I hadn't introduced myself to the lady nor intruded on her privacy. The gesture of an extravagant introvert, the result, I reasoned, of being in lockdown for so long.

Back in my suite, I took off my jacket and tie and donned a dark red robe. I felt warm and comfortable, having eaten lightly, and drunk a glass of Chasselas, the local wine grown on the terraces around Lake Geneva. I sat on one of the long blue sofas, admired my velvet monogrammed slippers then turned to gaze at the lake and mountains. I was happy to be on vacation.

I imagined the woman sipping champagne and marveling at the anonymous gift. I wondered if I would see her again. Perhaps in the lobby tomorrow or in the café later in the day or walking by the lake. Would she know me if she had, as I suspected, bribed the sommelier to tell her who had sent over the bottle?

People meet me then forget I exist. I blend into the surroundings, never one to stand out or pose a threat. I could be near a target with a small video camera on the table and they would take no notice of me. If I was seen with a beautiful woman, they would think I was extremely rich, for she could not have been attracted to my looks.

Slivers of moonlight broke across the waves on the lake as I stood by the window in my bedroom. I was reminded of Chekhov and his famous story *The Lady and the Lapdog*. The male character, Dmitri Dmitrich Gurov, seduced Anna Sergeyevna. Should I have approached the lone diner and asked if she was enjoying the champagne? Too late now. I was nothing like Dmitri. I had always been timid when it came to my personal life and the opposite sex.

I kicked off my slippers, threw off my dressing gown, brushed my teeth, washed my face, combed my mustache, and slid into the most comfortable sheets. I would have pondered how much I had missed luxury hotels, but I passed out.

.   .   .

I heard a tentative knock, not the usual sound of my room service man or whatever he was called. I donned my robe and adjusted the sash to hide my stomach. I returned to the bedroom to put on my slippers, the floor was cold. When I opened the door, I came face to face with the woman from the restaurant. In high heels, she was my height. She held a bucket of ice with the champagne bottle in one hand and two fluted glasses in the other. My mouth was wide open. I should have been mesmerized by my unexpected guest, but instead, I was fascinated by the etched pattern on the glasses.

"Are you going to let me in? This is bloody heavy," she whispered with a mischievous grin. I stepped aside and she marched into the main room and set the bucket on a small table between the two sofas.

"Please, make yourself at home." I meant to sound polite, not sarcastic.

She sat on one of the sofas and I sat beside her; I had a thousand questions but did not know where to begin.

I made sure my sash was secured then ran my hands through my messy hair. I knew my mustache was in order.

"Thank you. I'm also staying here. Not as long as you, though. Or as fancy." She surveyed the suite.

"How did you find me?" Her brocaded jacket was unbuttoned, and I caught a glimpse of her sheer lilac blouse. Her black hair glistened. Her eyes were very dark and shone. She wore thick mascara, had a straight nose, and full crimson lips. She was plump but in a sexy, natural way.

"Really? You have to ask me that? It's Switzerland. Everything's for sale here. Besides, I was intrigued by the man who bought me the most expensive champagne I've ever tasted." She turned her head to one side. "You still don't get it?" She paused. "The sommelier?"

"I saw you slipped him something."

"Yes. Here, we shouldn't waste it."

She poured two generous glasses, holding the bottle by its heel, and handed me one. I am suspicious if someone pours me a drink while they grasp the neck. It would be so easy to slip a crushed Rohypnol as they pour. I did not think she was the type to slip me a roofie, but her London accent did throw me, more Cockney than Oxford.

I held my glass up to the light and admired the bubbles, before I took a sip. It was heaven. Who had I sent the bottle to? I was about to find out. Her whole face glowed as she smacked her lips. I felt intoxicated.

"So, who are you to send over such a bottle and not follow with an invitation or a table visit? It was a bit rude don't you think? Anti-social?" She raised her eyebrows.

I scrunched mine. She didn't know me well enough to tease me.

"Everyone calls me Hud, short for Hudson." I ran my thumb and forefinger over my mustache, something I try to avoid, as it shows I am nervous.

She told me her name was Sophie, and as she leaned over to shake my hand, I became flustered and did not catch her last name. She had a firm dry grip. There was strength and confidence in her handshake that could be thrilling, or terrifying. I decided thrilling.

"I took you to be more Steve McQueen than Paul Newman," she threw back at me. Was she referring to Paul Newman the bad boy in *Hud*? No one had ever compared me to my two childhood heroes. I looked nothing like Paul Newman or Steve McQueen.

"Not Roderick Hudson?" I raised my eyebrows. It was my turn to tease her. I hated *Roderick Hudson* and didn't know why I recalled the name other than the schoolyard bullying I suffered when I read that damned novel.

"You're not Henry James' great-grandson, are you?"

I shook my head. So she was teasing me. I was not aware Henry James had any grandchildren. I tried to frown; I was supposed to be an expert in family trees.

I caught the scent of her perfume. I didn't recognize it. I prided myself in being able to identify the most popular perfumes. But here I was stymied, the result of my enforced isolation, I reasoned. It slowly came from her body like a mysterious drug. There were hints of lavender, citrus, and musk with an undertone of an exotic type of vanilla. I watched her chest as she breathed in and out and wondered if I was hallucinating.

"Are you a fan of Henry James?"

The question brought me back to reality. Was she talking in code?

"Not in this century." I went for the safe answer.

"What do you do, Hud? You must be doing well to be staying in this suite for three weeks."

She had done her homework, and I could see she eyed my robe and the rich pattern.

"Two weeks." I let out a sigh and gulped another mouthful of golden bubbles. "I'm an investigator. But not here. I'm on vacation. Or as you say holiday."

"A private eye?"

"Very private. No website. I don't advertise and I avoid the media. I have a very select clientele. Rich people have expensive problems. Why I can afford to stay here." I waved my glass in an expansive gesture, so out of character for me. The watch sparkled from the overhead lights. I was not going to tell her a client paid for the suite.

"And very discreet?"

I nodded and sipped my champagne. By now I had no idea if she was making fun of me or just being playful. I checked my mustache with my index finger. I saw her looking at my wrist.

"That's a nice watch. Is it a Royal Oak?"

"Yes. From a client."

"For a job well done?"

"Yes." I took another small sip and smiled at her, relieved she did not mention its value.

"Are you a fan of Nabokov? He lived here for ages, didn't he?" She turned around as if she could see his ghost.

"Was it this hotel or the other one? Anyway, not this suite." Maybe she had read the same online stories, or she was confused about the hotel? "He had Peter Ustinov pacing up and down over his head, and it drove him crazy, so he moved to the top floor," I added, pointing to the ceiling, playing along. Now I was confused as to the hotel Nabokov had stayed in.

"All that money he made from *Lolita* and the film rights." She squinted. "Did you like *Lolita*?"

Was she talking in code again? First, she had referred to Henry James as she eyed my sumptuous dressing gown, my monogrammed slippers, my full mustache. Did she think I was a homosexual? And now what was she inferring? That I liked young girls? What Nabokov called nymphet love repulsed me, but I know from all the interviews I've conducted in my career that someone protesting their innocence too much appears guilty, even if they are not. "I read it a long time ago." I paused to gauge her reaction, a minuscule tightening of her eyes and mouth. "I prefer a more mature woman." Her lips relaxed into a smile. I wanted to say *with a more ample figure* but thought that was going too far.

I had been reading *Lolita* when she walked past me. Before I had ordered the champagne, I had come to the part where Humbert Humbert had attempted to drug Lolita. The book, which I had bought here in Montreux, was not how I remembered it. I couldn't see the humor in violating a child. And the writing was too contrived for my taste. I write clear, simple reports. But I'm one of those readers who once I start a book, I have to finish it. Like a bad case, I must complete the investigation. Now, I thought of quitting the book and realized with horror that the book was splayed open on my bedside table.

"And I suppose you're not going to regale me with daring tales of your investigations of the extremely rich?"

"Well, let's see. Pour me another glass." She did and I looked at her as I sipped my drink. "I usually don't talk about my cases, but this is a perfect story I cannot resist telling you. But you have to promise never to repeat this? Promise?"

"I swear I won't tell a soul." She moved her stubby fingers up and down her chest and smiled.

"Have you heard of 'Friends of the Bees'? They have great T-shirts and caps."

"Yes. I've seen them."

"My client made a couple of small donations to the cause. He was approached by this con artist, let's call him the Count. Now the Count had presented to my client a very detailed proposal for the money he was about to receive, and my client was enthusiastic about saving the bees from pesticides and other environmental hazards. Then late one night the Count emails and then calls my client in a panic. His biggest sponsor had been threatened by a multinational and had pulled out, days before a rollout of a new program to save the bees throughout Europe. He pleaded with my client to make an emergency loan of the money and he would be paid back in a month once other financing had come through from a rival multinational. It just so happened my client knew the rival multinational, he was a major shareholder, so he wired the Count the money the next morning." I took a mouthful of champagne. I had forgotten when I had last talked so much.

"How much?"

"It was supposed to be a million Euros but later that day my client was notified his wire for ten million had gone through."

"Ten million Euros?"

"Yes."

She put her lips together and whistled. "So, what did you do?"

"By the time I contacted his bank with my client's authorization, the money had been disbursed around the world and was untraceable. At least according to the bank's fraud department. So before my client set his lawyers on the bank, I did some more digging and discovered the charity operated under another name, Greeneland Enterprises. It wasn't even a listed charity."

"Aren't you supposed to do due diligence for your clients? And prevent this sort of thing?"

"That's just it. Ordinarily, I would, but he thought the original sums he gave the Count too small to bother me with. It turns out all the illustrious members of Friends of the Bees board were the Count's alter egos. Count Wormald from Monaco, as chairman, of course, Monsignor Duran from Madrid, Jonathan Rickards from Mayfair, and Col. John Sutro from Texas. The website, everything disappeared the next day. He must have planned this in detail."

"So, did you find him?"

I gave her my close-lipped triumphant smile and stroked my mustache. "Of course." I took my time emptying my glass.

"Are you going to tell me?"

"Strictly confidential. Right? You cannot tell anyone."

"Cross my heart." She repeated the movement with her fingers over her chest.

"I managed to find his I.P. address in the original source code of his email and he made the mistake of using his home in Monaco. I raced there and discovered his rented apartment was vacant."

"How did you get into the building? They're very security conscious there."

"I do have a certain authority as an investigator, and a few hundred Euros certainly opens doors. I searched his apartment and of course, people always leave something behind. I found a torn slip of paper with a long list of numbers, an empty water bottle under the sink, and a disgusting piece of underwear I bagged for DNA. Then the building gave me screenshots of his face as he entered and exited the foyer, as well as his rental agreement. He had provided his French identity card with an address in Paris. So, I flew to Paris."

"You must have a nice expense account."

"It's a fact you have to spend money to find money. Once I realized the identity card was fake, I checked the address on his card. Again, it was a dead end. No one of that name had ever lived there although the concierge did remember one of the names, I gave her. She could not confirm the photo I showed her. She was pretending to earn her hundred Euros, which was okay. Next stop was Jacques."

"Jacques?"

"Yes. I like to say as an investigator you are only as good as your sources and Jacques was in some Police department in Paris with a long name I cannot pronounce. I presented him everything I had in one of those long French lunches with lots of wine. Jacques was on the trail of the Count as well, though he knew him as a Harold Lime if you can believe that."

"Goodness."

"With the fingerprints and photo recognition, we found his real identity. The DNA results would be too late, but wouldn't you know it he was in Paris in a small hotel right next to a famous brothel. Jacques and his team picked him up that night. The Count had several Red Notices, you know from Interpol, under different names and disguises, and the French were very interested in him as well."

"Well, did you get the money?"

"He had a private jet ready to take him to Malta the next morning and yes, he made a deal where he gave up my client's money in return for leniency for all the other crimes they were accusing him of."

"You mean your Jacques had the authority to make such a deal?"

"His superiors approved the deal. Don't underestimate the political influence my client has in France."

"Oh, I get it. That is an amazing tale."

"Yes. Just goes to show if you spend enough money on an investigation, you can get results. But what about you? You seem to have a literary focus. You're in publishing?"

"Oh, you are good. I used to work for one of the big five but a few years ago formed my own literary agency. No regrets."

"Big five?"

"Yes, five." She held her hand up, palm facing me. "The biggest publishing companies. They're really conglomerates and have a monopoly on publishing."

"Oh. Sounds like a cartel to me." I knew about criminal organizations but what did I understand about publishing? I took another sip of champagne and nodded my head as if I knew what I was talking about, a trait I was particularly good at. And I thought my mustache gave me added gravitas. "But you're here to snag a new client?"

"Again, you're right on the money." Her voice dropped to a whisper. "I'm trying to be discreet as well. She's a best-selling author, unhappy with her agent."

"So, you can't visit with a hooker, a bag of coke, and a bottle of bubbly?" I remembered an art dealer from New York telling me how she had claimed her prize painter with a similar strategy. A limo, a bag of coke, and a good-looking hooker and the male artist signed on the dotted line. I felt I could say anything to her, using my fake English accent, as I waved my fluted glass in the air.

"You do a London accent rather well. Americans when they try to be British usually sound like Benny Hill."

"That's a name I haven't heard in a long time. I take it you're based in London? You grew up there?"

"Yes." She placed her glass carefully on the low table in front of us, and I noticed her long red nails. I had not registered this detail when she made her dramatic entrance into the restaurant. How could I be so unobservant? Then again this was the first time I'd had a woman in my hotel room, correction, suite.

"I'm the living embodiment of Samuel Johnson's famous quote about London. But your earlier comment got me thinking. I don't know if she bats for the other side, or if she does drugs. I know she drinks, so I'll go with the bottle of champagne. To celebrate switching agents. Yes!" She slapped her hands on her robust thighs and I saw her nail polish matched the red embroidery on the cuff of my gown. We were almost knee to knee on the sofa.

"I'd say you live in a much nicer neighborhood now than you grew up in. Must've been hell going through your lockdown. Your leaders didn't do so well, did they?" I gave my empathic frown and leaned toward her. She shook her head.

"I want to forget about the whole thing. Don't want to even mention it." She emptied the bottle into our glasses.

"I agree. Where do you live now? Somewhere very posh, but not Sloane Square or Mayfair." I wanted to be right about my observations. Despite being isolated for so long, I could still read people. "Probably near Harrods or Harvey Nicks as you call it."

"Yes. You're right, Knightsbridge. Near Harrods."

"Of course." I nodded. "I know London well." I was going to comment about the Saudis in her neighborhood or Julian Assange who had been a prisoner in the Ecuador Embassy adjacent to Harrods but decided not to. Perhaps she had some Arab blood in her, which made her appear exotic. "Always so much to see and do though I haven't been there for two years with all this." I waved my glass and dared not be more specific.

She nodded. "Where do you stay?"

"At the Stafford, a Mews suite. It's very English but central. They know me there. It's my home in London and near all the shopping."

"You bought your gown on Bond Street?" She touched the cuff and for a moment I panicked, then smiled and checked my mustache again with thumb and forefinger.

"Jermyn Street."

"And you live in the States?"

"Florida. Miami Beach. In a condo by the ocean. It's a place where I store my stuff. I travel a lot. Well, I used to travel."

"Not near where that building collapsed?"

"No, thank goodness. Let's not talk about bad things. Do you have plans for tomorrow? Can I take you to a delightful little restaurant in Lausanne? Graham Greene used to eat there if we're still doing literary connections."

"You are the clever one aren't you, and I'd be honored. Only I might have to take a client out to dinner. Can I let you know later in the afternoon? I don't want to break my promise." Then in the silence, it was her turn to nod her head. "Graham Greene? I didn't think anyone still read him."

I wasn't going to admit he was my favorite author, and I identified with his sad, broken characters. My thoughts disturbed the spell as we looked at each other. I was tired and needed my sleep. Was Sophie expecting more from me? I was unsure what she wanted. She hadn't stroked my dressing gown sleeve again, a gesture I had found unexpected and thrilling.

If I had watched more romantic movies in my youth, I would have held her stubby fingers in my hand, kissed them as I looked into her eyes, and told her how enchanted I was she had come to my suite. I would have paused, still holding her hand, to gauge her reaction. Then, I don't know what I would have done, I was never confident with the opposite sex. The entire scene had an air of illusion, a midwinter dream.

Instead, I asked if she needed anything else before I rose from the sofa and put my hand to my mouth. It wasn't a very convincing yawn, but she got the message.

"And here's my phone number." I wrote it on a piece of hotel stationery and handed it to her. "I'm using a rented phone here. Left my phone in a Faraday cage so no one could track me and bought this at a local shop, not the airport where they can link facial recognition, my name, and flight number with a rented phone."

"They? Are you on the run?" she asked playfully.

"I don't want anyone tracking me."

"You are technically minded." She remained on the sofa and checked her glass before taking a final sip. She fixed me with her eyes as she swallowed and smacked her lips.

"More paranoid than technical. And you could have been sent by someone to check me out."

She leaned forward to ease herself off the sofa and adjusted her pants. "You're the one who sent me the bottle." By taking a step towards me I thought for a moment she was going to place her hands on my shoulders.

"I must admit I am a little stressed even if I'm on vacation." I adjusted my sash and looked at her. I've never had a beautiful woman come to my suite with a bottle of champagne, even if I had paid for it.

"Perhaps you need to relax and unwind." She was now so close to me I could inhale her perfume, like a drug. I froze, then the moment was gone. I took a step back and she followed me to the door.

"I was going to take the train to the chocolate factory but I'm not sure if it's running. Everyone here seems to be mad about skiing, even though it's late in the season I'm told. Do you ski?"

"Not since my accident, and I'll have to wait and see with my new client."

I was now at the entrance to the suite and held the door open for her. This was my cue to ask about her skiing accident, but I let it pass. She didn't ask if I skied. I obviously didn't have the type of body you would see on the slopes. She stood close to me again and smiled. I inhaled her scent one last time and closed my eyes for a second. Emboldened by the alcohol, I gave her a quick peck on the cheek.

"Thank you for tracking me down. As you can imagine I don't have people finding me when I want to remain hidden." How could I sound so pretentious? Her perfume had gone to my head.

"And thank you for the champagne. I had a very pleasant and unusual evening." For a moment she stayed next to me, and I wondered if something would happen. I'm not one to start kissing a woman I've just met, on both cheeks, even if we were on the French side of Switzerland. I wondered what she meant by unusual, as I watched her walk to the elevator swinging her hips.

.   .   .

Light flooded my bedroom when I opened my eyes. *Lolita* was by my bedside, and so was my cheap phone. I checked my surroundings as I stumbled into the living room. There was no sign of a champagne bottle, ice bucket, or fluted glasses. There was no pen or notepad either. I opened the door of my suite and checked the empty corridor.

I closed the door and saw an envelope on the floor. Inside was the bill for the champagne I had charged to my room along with the generous tip. I had misread the decimal point. It was very expensive champagne. I realized I couldn't stay here.

I sat on the sofa, ran my thumb and forefinger over my mustache, and tried to imagine her scent.

AMANDA, GOYA, ST. FRANCIS, JONI MITCHELL, and MA BELL

DON'T REACH OUT AND DON'T TOUCH

The joy of being with someone, the surprise of a chance encounter that leads to an adventure, the delight in catching up with an old friend, were all lost in lockdowns, social distancing, and the compulsory wearing of masks that hid smiles.

We were deprived of basic human contact.

THE OTHER 1984

1/1/1984 was the date set by the Federal Government for the breakup of Ma Bell, also known as the Bell System, AT&T, or the Telephone Company. Their monopoly over all telephone and data transmissions, the telephone in your house, and the wiring and mechanical switches and computers that controlled them, came to an end on that date. The Bell System had invented and spent millions advertising the jingle to encourage people to use the telephone.

REACH OUT AND TOUCH SOMEONE

You had to use Ma Bell. Now you didn't.

BACK IN 1984

We had no idea the liberation of voice and data communications from Ma Bell's monopoly would lead to the birth of the internet. Nor could we envisage the spawning of different and vastly larger monopolies that would influence and control our lives both positively and negatively. Nor could we have imagined the amount of money to be made from breaking up the phone company.

DIGITAL DREAMS

In 1983 I had a clear view of the Statue of Liberty and the Hudson River from my office window at the computer telephone integration company I worked for. I designed digital voicemail trees and other systems that we did not have the technology to implement.

THE DISMANTLING OF THE COMMUNICATION MONOPOLY

At the first conference on the breakup of the Bell System, I accompanied our Chief Financial Officer to the St. Francis Hotel in San Francisco. We shared a two-bedroom corner suite on the top floor overlooking Union Square. The Presidential Suite was huge. I had no idea how the CFO obtained the suite, but my company worked on a grand scale, so I took the booking for granted.

The conference attendees were almost exclusively male engineers and pole climbers. Pole climber was a title we gave to cable operators who started out climbing poles to install their TV and phone service. It reflected their restricted outlook on new technology as they were used to stringing cables from pole to pole. I recall only one presenter telling a joke and no one laughed. The audience had no idea what was in store for them, how we were on the cusp of a digital revolution that would change the world. In fairness to the engineers and pole climbers, few computers existed, and telephone switches were analog, not digital. Everything was slower, more expensive, and immune to fast change. We did not know that in a few years the internet would transform the world.

AMANDA AND HER FIRST PORNO FILM

I met Amanda in New York a few months earlier and we shared interests in books and films. At the time I had several female friends. Not girlfriends, just buddies I could hang out with. She was a film buddy. I took her to her first porn movie in the Village. The two other couples there ran into the bathrooms once the film got interesting and made a lot of noise. We could hear both couples from our seats. We diligently watched the entire movie like French New Wave film buffs. Amanda was fascinated. I was bored. After we parted. I rushed uptown to see my girlfriend. Amanda took the train to her boyfriend in New Jersey.

Amanda was going to be in San Francisco when I was at this conference. We arranged to meet. Only I forgot. Before cell phones, if you had not made plans, linking up could be a challenge. There were a lot of people waiting under clocks, or on street corners. Amanda, a young student who exhibited a take-charge attitude, came to the St. Francis and knocked on my door. She was impressed by my suite. We started drinking from the well-stocked bar sitting across from each other in large armchairs. A few years before, Joni Mitchell had written her song "Real Good for Free" in the same suite, I told Amanda.

ALL NIGHT LONG

Later, we decided to take in the sights. Why spend all night drinking in a luxurious hotel suite when San Francisco after dark was calling us? We walked to City Lights

Bookstore where I bought *Howl* by Allen Ginsberg. I had given away my copy. I wanted to read it to Amanda. I found the latest Richard Brautigan novel I had not read, *Dreaming of Babylon*, about an incompetent private detective set in San Francisco in 1942. Perfect for me. I could identify with him. We paid a visit to Carol Doda at the Condor Club, and we were not impressed with her breasts. We had dinner in Chinatown before returning to the hotel. Being with Amanda was relaxing even though she was bubbling over with energy and ideas. There was no tension between us. She had a boyfriend back in New Jersey she said she loved. I had a girlfriend in New York I was keen on but could not admit I was in love with.

JAMES BOND vs THE GREEN LIGHT THEORY

I grew up seeing forceful male role models in movies, like the early James Bond. His behavior was confusing to a randy teenager. Bond operated in the gray area between consent and coercion, between seduction and rape. Bond's attitude was he was irresistible to women, even if they did resist. They would succumb to his strong will, his physical force, and his overbearing masculine charm. After I got my face slapped a couple of times, I realized I was not James Bond.

In time, I understood women gave you subtle hints as to whether they wanted the relationship to become more intimate, or not. I became a firm believer in the green light theory. It had nothing to do with film financing, a term not invented back in the 1980s. The green light theory is based on how a woman signals to a man how far he can go. Men usually play catch-up, as we do not understand the subtle cues a woman is giving us.

Sometimes the green light appears, then flickers, and disappears. Sometimes it is never turned on. It can be confusing for both the sensitive and the thick male.

THE UNCERTAINTY PRINCIPLE

No matter the cues, for the male there is always uncertainty. Do you make a move or don't you? Imagine it is late at night, you've had dinner together, and you are getting on like a house on fire. Do you make a move, and if rejected, is the relationship over? Or do you decide not to make a move and she becomes mad at you because you rejected her? And the relationship is over. Either way, you cannot win. Hence the green light theory. But it might not work, for if the woman does not know about the green light, does not supply you with any cues, and you are left clueless as to her desire for intimacy, then what? The male could be equally clueless as to how to read the subtle physical and verbal hints the woman is feeding him.

NO GREEN LIGHT BUT SHE WAS NAKED

I do not remember how Amanda finished up naked on my king-sized bed in the corner suite of the St. Francis Hotel. She told me again about her boyfriend back in New Jersey, and how she had to remain true to him. There was no green light. Her knees were locked together. I looked everywhere in that corner suite at the St. Francis, but I could not find the green light, only her stark nakedness on my bed. I found out later, the night she was lying next to me, naked with her knees pressed together, her boyfriend had been with her best friend and the green light had been on.

Neither of us could sleep. She reminded me of Francisco Goya's *Naked Maja*, only better looking, with creamy white skin, large breasts, and curly hair that fell below her shoulders. I definitely wanted to reach out and touch her, she looked so ravishing. There was no green light.

BREAKFAST AT ENRICO'S

When we saw sunlight appear through our windows we got dressed and walked to Enrico's on Broadway to have breakfast. Pancakes, eggs, toast, and coffee. Lots of coffee. We felt elated. In all our excitement I had forgotten to read her *Howl*. I couldn't imagine shouting the poem naked, as I jumped up and down on the bed, while Amanda was sprawled beneath me with her legs pressed together, would have gone over too well.

There was a brightness to our consciousness, having stayed up all night. The world appeared sharper, and more intense and our bodies were relaxed and more open. Maybe we were just tired, but we could not have been exhausted as we hadn't done anything. We held hands as friends, not lovers, as we walked back to the hotel. I had another day of humorless engineers talking about the breakup of Ma Bell.

I returned to New York and gazed at the Statue of Liberty from my office chair. I thought about the green light, and how to design a voicemail system for a digital telephone that had not been invented. I never went out with Amanda again and wondered if I had misread her signals. Perhaps the green light theory was flawed, and she was annoyed at me for spending the night with her, naked, in the corner suite of the St. Francis Hotel. And I had not read her *Howl* as promised.

Converting from analog to digital was not going to be easy.

> *Never trust a writer, they make stuff up.*
> *Trust an investigator, they collect facts.*
> Peter T. Barnes, P.I.

In "Real Good for Free", Joni Mitchell sings how she had slept the previous night in the Fairmont Hotel. At the time, I thought this was the St. Francis in San Francisco. The song was recorded live at the Berkeley Community Theater on March 2nd, 1974. The track was included in her best-selling album *Miles of Aisles*. Our hotel was the Westin St. Francis Hotel on Union Square. The Fairmont Hotel where Joni Mitchell had stayed was on Nob Hill.

While researching the reference to the hotel, I emailed the archivist of the Joni Mitchell website. He sent me a story that was featured in the *East Village Other* on March 17th, 1970. 'Blind Richie', who was a heroin addict on the lower East Side in Manhattan, had lost his clarinet and now begged on a street corner. There were additional stories in the Joni Mitchell archive about how she had heard him playing his clarinet on a street corner in Manhattan and had been inspired to write the song, "Real Good for Free".

I could have regaled Amanda with true stories about the St. Francis and our suite: how Fatty Arbuckle was accused of murdering a young actress Virginia Rappe (her first silent film role in 1917 was in *The Foolish Virgin*), in the bedroom where we lay naked, Amanda's knees pressed together, or how Al Jolson dropped dead of a heart attack while playing cards, where we were drinking from the well-stocked bar, or how President Ford was almost shot outside the hotel by Sara Jane Moore in 1975.

Sometimes it is better to make stuff up. No one is going to remember the details anyway.

Never trust a writer of fiction.

AN EIGHTEENTH-CENTURY
LOVE PROBLEM

An Interesting Problem by Adolphe Alexandre Lesrel (1839–1929)

"You can solve a chess problem, but you cannot solve a love problem."

Adolphe Alexandre Lesrel (1839–1929) was well known in his time as a French academic who specialized in seventeenth-century genre paintings featuring jovial gentlemen in fine pursuits, drinking wine and beer, selecting a sword, or enjoying each other's company. He also portrayed women in mythological or highly romanticized poses. But this Parisian aristocrat's portrait is different. Quiet and contemplative, it tells a multi-layered tale we can only interpret using the clues in the painting.

Lesrel's gentleman looks decidedly modern despite the white wig. Clean-shaven, unlike other Lesrel men with their goatees, longer wigs, and flamboyant clothes, our chess player's brocaded jacket is undone. He contemplates a chess board, playing himself. But what is missing from the picture, other than an opponent and several chess pieces? First, there is no violin bow. His violin is discarded against the chair on which rests an upturned hat. Was he going out or has he just returned? He looks like he has been in the room for some time. What are the clues?

Obviously, the violin. He was playing before throwing the bow out of the picture. He has a few books and a notebook open on the floor. He has written a letter, maybe several attempts at a letter, for one quill is discarded on the floor while the other is in its holder. Perhaps he has composed letters like Valmont in *Les Liaisons Dangereuses*. His amorous strategy is unknown to us, as he is waiting for a reply, but the reply has not arrived. He looks frustrated and impatient, and he does not know his next move. Do we really care about his chess problem or are we only imagining his love problem? Checkmate or lovemate? Or are we confusing an affair with a love affair, confusing sexual conquest with romantic love?

Will she summon the chess player to her house or is she already entertaining another lover? What of the gentleman's wife? Is he married? He wears no wedding ring. In all the paintings I have seen by Lesrel of this period, he never paints rings on any male fingers. Is this historically accurate? Or could he not be bothered to paint rings? The chess player is of an age when he would be successfully married into Parisian society, for status, wealth, and political strategy.

According to Francine Du Plessix Gray in her brilliant book *At Home with the Marquis De Sade*, we learn French aristocracy at that time would never be in love or faithful to their spouses.

Perhaps his wife is enjoying herself with an afternoon of adulterous pursuits elsewhere, thinking her husband is doing the same? I estimate it is the afternoon. A gentleman does not rise too early in the day. There are no drinks on the table, nor is there lunch or food visible. It's too early to light candles but not too late to visit a lover in his day coat.

And what of the faded tapestry that takes up over half the painting? Does the mythical and idyllic scene comment on, or yield clues to our chess player's woes? The pastoral scene is in sharp contrast to the live tableau below: urban frustration and deliberation, and perhaps deception. What of the fact there are fewer chess pieces on the board and table than are necessary to play a game? Did Lesrel know how to play chess? Or did he give up adding chess pieces?

Another dimension to consider with this painting is its small size. The canvas is a mere 14″ × 10.8″ or 35.5 cm by 27.5 cm. Reproduced digitally, the painting feels much larger, not life-size but at least four feet high. Why did Lesrel paint such small paintings? Were they more commercially acceptable?

Our chess player is waiting for a reply to a letter. If he appears in society, there will be gossip as to why he is out and not with his wife or his lover. Perhaps he lives in the time of the publication of *Point de Lendemain* (*No Tomorrow*), a novella by Dominque Vivant Denon, a masterpiece of intrigue and understated sensuality, published in 1779.

Is our chess player part of an elaborate game?

He faces a difficult problem but, like us, he sits in solitude, at home. At least he is not under lockdown orders or facing a pandemic.

DAISY CROWN

She knelt beside me in her Chinese dress and threaded daisies over my head. We were in Albert Park on a quiet spring afternoon, between the bandstand and the Queen Victoria statue. Bridget did not say much. I was content to do nothing but watch her play with daisies and bask in her presence.

Bridget had run away from home when she turned eighteen with her twin sister Moira and worked in a massage parlor in Kings Cross, Sydney. She did not talk about her experiences there and I never asked for a massage. The sisters reconciled with their parents and returned to their posh Remuera home with a swimming pool perched on a cliff.

Bridget and Moira helped me form an art rock group. They could not sing but neither could I. We rehearsed for weeks and learned four songs I had written for a performance in an art space. They had an exuberant stage presence and in their micro dresses the twins, and their best friend who was a day younger, were visually stunning. I sang and played guitar, the girls provided chorus and backup, and we had an acne-scarred teenage boy who filled out the sound with a synthesizer and drum machine.

At our last performance, the crowd became hysterical, and we had to repeat our meager repertoire three times. I realized the audience did not listen to the music so much as responded to the visceral energy we produced by our stage image and antics. I am grateful there are no recordings of our performances. We must have sounded awful.

At the park after our rock career, we were hanging out and enjoying each other's company with no demands, no deep conversation, and no plans.

As we get older, we do not enjoy such moments. There is too much emphasis on using our time wisely, always checking our smartphones, and maintaining a busy schedule, as if this bustle of activities gives meaning to our lives.

Having survived the pandemic, we should be able to relax more and enjoy peace and tranquility with the people we love.

A LOVE STORY about a
FORTUNATE BOOK

I read Richard Brautigan's last novel about a woman who had hung herself and how he had slept in her bed in that house in San Francisco. *An Unfortunate Woman* was published in the US sixteen years after his suicide in 1984.

My copy is marked DISCARD from the Irvington Public Library. The red stamped letters are on the front of the book, on the fore edge, and in the back above the date due insert. According to the date stamps it was lent out in 2000 when it was published, once in 2001, and then after a thirteen-year hiatus again in 2014, the last time anyone borrowed it. All three times took place in August, the height of the summer in Irvington-on-Hudson, New York. Good summer reading for three people in Irvington-on-Hudson.

Librarians discard books that are not read to make way for newer more popular books. We can assume three people read this book over those fourteen years. Now I have a first edition in excellent condition other than the red stamps marking the book a discard. The book is finally in good hands.

An online search of the Irvington Public Library reveals there are still three copies of *An Unfortunate Woman* available within the Westchester Library System. One is in Larchmont Public Library; one is in Mount Vernon Public Library, and one is in White Plains Library. All ten of his other novels, some poetry, and biographies are also available. You reserve the books online to get the copies delivered to your library. Richard Brautigan is well cared for in the Westchester Library System

NIKOLAI NIKOLAEVICH and ANNA SERGEYEVNA, SIBLING LOVE, MOSCOW STYLE

WHAT HAPPENED AFTER THE JADED SPY

The Order of Lenin

The characters of *The Jaded Trilogy* lived on in my mind during the lockdown. I wondered what would happen to the Soviet spy, Nikolai Nikolaevich Raganovich when he left Wellington to return to Moscow. The spy scandal and trial of the famous N.Z. economist Doctor Summer was included in *The Jaded Spy,* as was his nemesis Nikolai Nikolaevich Raganovich.

"Did you think you were going to be so…" Colonel Anna Sergeyevna Raganovich struggled for the correct word in English, as she poured vodka into his glass, then her own. "So well received?"

She held her vodka glass to her thin lips, her eyes fixed on him. Her dyed black hair was shorter than her brother had remembered. She wore no earrings or make-up and with her big ears and long nose, she looked menacing until she focused her cold fisheyes on him, then she was terrifying. She was so short her knee-length boots barely touched the carpet.

Nikolai Nikolaevich Raganovich could only nod his head, once. He had allowed his once ample but now thinner body to sink into the other armchair in her living room. He was still slowly warming to his sister in her KGB uniform and her new look. Well, half-sister. They had the same mother. Colonel Anna had shown up at the small ceremony in the Kremlin, which was propitious, as he wanted to stay at her apartment until he had sorted out his accommodation. She wore her full complement of medals, hiding what little she had in the way of a chest.

They continued to speak in English, to practice their conversational techniques. He had lost count of the men Anna Sergeyevna had dated who had referred to her first name and patronymic, in an attempt to joke about Anton Chekhov. Each had been shipped to Siberia. He could not imagine her with a lap dog, or any pet, other than a black widow spider.

"I spent three weeks in a dacha being debriefed. That's the word they use now. Sounds very Western. It felt like an interrogation." He ran his hands over his newer woolen suit trousers and looked at his wrists that bore no markings. He had thrown away his shiny pants and jacket from the dacha. His new leather shoes, a little too large for his feet, held their polish.

He could have been taken to the Aquarium, the GRU's headquarters. Even though his sister worked for the KGB, he knew she had enough power to have him traded to their rival Red Army intelligence agency, to be tied to a wooden plank and fed into the furnace in the basement of the Aquarium. He had heard such stories about his sister and had seen the film clips that inspired loyalty to Mother Russia and fear of the Soviet State. He was thankful he had not embarked on a short film career.

After his interrogation, a quick execution in the basement of Lubyanka, in the KGB prison, would be better than being transported to Siberia. Instead, he was given a suit before leaving the dacha and driven to the Kremlin where he received the Order of Lenin. The clothes were probably from an agent who had been shot, an irony that did not escape him.

"They were being thorough, but they did not harm you. Correct?"

"It wasn't Lubyanka, but it wasn't a health spa either. Look how much weight I lost." He patted his flat stomach. "I suppose I have you to thank." He ran his hands through his short red hair and looked at his intact fingers and fingernails. He would never eat cabbage soup again.

His sister crinkled her nose and Nikolai did not know how to interpret the gesture.

"Are you ever going to take that medal off?"

"It's a reminder of what your humble younger brother has accomplished serving Mother Russia, Comrade Colonel." Nikolai Nikolaevich clapped his hands on his knees and then looked at the high ceiling. After being strapped to a chair for so long, he was surprised he still had feeling in his legs.

"Oh, you can cut the crap, Nikolai. There is no recording here in my apartment. Remember I supervised the wiring." She waved her hand to imply all the Kotelnicheskaya Embankment apartments were bugged, one of the elite buildings Stalin had built near the Kremlin.

Nikolai took another sip of his vodka and looked at the bottle on the low table between them. His sister sat opposite. He was relieved she did not refer to him as Nikolai Nikolaevich. She only did that when she wanted to remind him of their different fathers.

"You were lucky you were not declared Persona Non-Grata. It would've hurt your record."

"I can always change my name. But you are correct. The Kiwis wanted to export their sheep to us and had a new ambassador here. They had to play the game. It's a wonder they only found out about the doctor. It took them so long."

"I hear they are not so smart."

"They have no understanding of our psychological operations. They are like the Americans. They see the world in black and white. It's about how men in power think and act, not the latest sheep births or the currency changes. The good Doctor Summer was influential to five of their prime ministers. Five." He held up the fingers on his left hand as if he had won five sports championships. "Our influence operations have had a profound effect on the New Zealanders. Look how anti-American they are now. They've banned US warships, and the US Navy no longer has a presence in the South Pacific. And they are nuclear-free. That can only help us, thanks in part to our special friends and others."

"Yes, the others." She moved her head slightly.

"It's a wonder they never found the others. By giving up the doctor, we saved the rest. You know they didn't even find our dead drops, or codes, or learn our methods of contact? They knew nothing of our techniques. So, we did fool them."

"What about your prize agent?"

"The former head of the Communist Youth Party?"

"Yes. Mark Rose. And don't look so surprised, I read the reports."

"One day Mark will be an important politician, his radical past forgotten. And he will be ours. Do you know he stole the mayor's office door and hung it in the university's student cafeteria? And he tried to tow a boat into their Navy yard. Loaded with gelignite. Some of which he had already used to sow confusion amongst the authorities there. They can certainly panic! Westerners are so weak.

Anyway, the boat sank along with the gelignite. It would have been spectacular if it had hit their one frigate and sunk it."

"They only have one frigate?"

"Yes. That's their Navy. The other frigate's boiler blew so they have only one battleship."

"Why did you get him to steal that painting? What was it? Some English explorer. A cook. Captain Cook."

"It was, how do I say it, mozhna?"

"You improvised," she stated. Her face was blank.

"Yes."

"The Kremlin was unhappy when they finally heard about your adventure."

"But it was resolved. I thought the stolen painting would finish up in the hands of a Māori Land Rights group. Then Wiremu Wilson, the ringleader, knocked on my door offering to sell me the notebooks. He even gave me a lecture on Marxism and land use." Nikolai Nikolaevich attempted a smile. "You heard of the notebooks?"

"Of course. We tried to get them in New York and were unsuccessful because some stupid female doctor beat up our Albanians."

"Weren't they Romanians? Or Bulgarians? I get confused."

"Who cares. We lost the books. But at least you got them, but at some price, I hear."

"Yes. And I copied them before the police illegally searched me and stole them."

"I hear the Americans got copies as well."

"You did?" Nikolai Nikolaevich acted surprised, then knew better than to ask how she would know such information. He looked up at the ceiling again then at the freestanding lamp in the corner. If there was one thing he knew about his sister, it was she was far from honest. In other words, parting with the truth pained her. But who was honest if you lived to survive in Mother Russia? He understood he had been tainted by his exposure to Western countries and their ideas of democracy and a free society. He had to get his mind back into the Soviet way of thinking, as if being strapped to a chair, injected with all sorts of chemicals, and being yelled at for three weeks with little sleep, had not done the trick. He stared at the vodka bottle, but his sister ignored his look.

"If the police had not illegally searched my daughter's apartment, I would have traded the painting for the notebooks, but it was too late. Those Māori are very subversive. They'll be running the country soon. The Kiwis there are too weak. My only regret was I did not finish that nuisance of a curator. He screwed up everything." He took a deep breath. "At least I caused his van to crash. He should have died. But I got copies of the notebooks and Mr. Rose is still operational, as are the others, whom I am sure you know of. So, it was a successful mission."

His sister did not respond. He looked at the vodka bottle. She scrutinized him. Nikolai Nikolaevich could not say anything else in case he incriminated himself or contradicted what he had stated in the dacha, under duress.

He finished his drink and slammed the glass on the table before leaning back to look at the ceiling. He caught himself and glanced at his sister.

"Did you tell Mr. Rose about the Order of Lenin waiting for him in the Kremlin?"

"Yes. Of course. I always use that story." Here he changed his voice to a deliberate Moscow accent. "There is a special Order of Lenin waiting for you with your name on it, in the

Kremlin." He looked at his sister to see if she would react. But she did not. "He believed me. They always do. They get so teary-eyed. What is it with Westerners? It's saved us millions of rubles!" When Nikolai laughed his lips moved sideways but his eyes remained dead.

"Who said communists don't have a sense of humor?" Her utterance surprised him, but he caught himself.

"I believe it was you." Nikolai waited for a response but remembered only his sister could tell jokes and laugh. All others had to be circumspect.

"How is your daughter, Natasha Windsor Raganovich?"

"Doing well in her studies. Although now they think she is, what they call a sleeper agent."

Here he was not upset about his daughter not using his patronymic, Nikolaevich, as they had agreed she should use her Russian mother's new name of Windsor, in keeping with her claim to be American with English ancestry.

"We can always move her to Australia. They're just as clueless."

"Yes. She'll like it there."

"You never answered my question. Are you going to keep wearing your medal?"

"Let's finish the bottle first." He waited for her to pour the rest into their glasses as she fixed him with her eyes.

"When you take off that medal you need to get your suit cleaned. You don't know where it's been."

He shuddered and made a note to check under his bed, and between the covers, to make sure no black widow was hiding in his room.

MEL COMES to the MOUNTAIN
or
CHEKHOV and MAYONNAISE

WHAT HAPPENED AFTER THE JADED WIDOW

View of Rangitoto from Maungawhau, formerly known as Mount Eden.

Richard Brautigan said he always wanted to write a book with the last word: mayonnaise. The novel was *Trout Fishing in America*.

"I always wanted to write a story including Chekhov and *Tristram Shandy*, make a cameo appearance as myself, and have 'mayonnaise' as the last word, to honor Richard Brautigan."
Nick Spill, sometime after *The Jaded Widow*.

Anton Chekhov wrote a short story called "Mayonnaise" in 1883, and it features a journalist called N.Z.

EXT. MT. EDEN PATH TO SUMMIT. DUSK.
On a cold, clear afternoon in August with fading light, two figures climbed a muddy track. They had taken the steps at the end of Rautangi Road. Alexander Newton is a tall broad-shouldered man in his late twenties and Dr. Mel Johnson is a slim athletic woman in her early thirties.

CUT TO:

MEL
Alex! Can you slow down?

ALEXANDER
Oh. It's Alex now? When you're mad at me?

MEL
I'm not mad. I just need to get your attention. I'm not so agile.

ALEXANDER
At least you're not calling me Sacha.
Then we'd be in a Chekhov short
story, and it would end badly.

Portrait of Anton Pavlovich Chekhov, 1898 by Osip Braz

MEL
Sadly, not badly. But so far, so good.
Here, help me.

ALEXANDER
It rained earlier. Mind your step.

Alexander helped Mel climb to the next grassy terrace. She
adjusted her long black dress and clicked her muddy Doc
Marten boots. From behind, in her black leather jacket,

she did not look five months pregnant. Alexander wore his denim jacket. He found the weather mild compared to Wellington and had run up the same track early in the morning before showering and heading to his job as cu-rator at the gallery. He had regained the feeling of fitness after his long recovery from his near-fatal accident and was now determined to enjoy the last months before he became a father and his life changed forever. He had read Dr. Spock's latest book and was determined to do the exact opposite, although if he was honest with himself, he would not have much say in the matter of child-rearing with Dr. Mel as mother. He might be relegated to nappy changing and bringing up wind, but he was still excited.

ALEXANDER
I'm glad we didn't pack a picnic, it's
too wet up here.

He took both of her hands and guided her to a flat spot in the trail. When they reached the carpark at the summit, the wind swept Mel's hair back and Alexander stopped to adjust a curl that fell over her eyes. He kissed her on the cheek and placed his left hand on her bump. Mel shivered.

MEL
It's cold.

Alexander ran his hands up and down her back, inside her jacket. The parking lot was full, and a tourist bus had parked by the steps to the Trig point.

ALEXANDER
It kicked me.

MEL

It?

ALEXANDER

It's a girl, isn't it? She's practicing her kung fu kicks.

MEL

I showed you the ultrasound. You made some comment about no penis. Remember?

ALEXANDER

Oh. Shall we go to the Rangitoto side?

MEL

Yes. Remember our picnic, the look on your face when you finally worked out why I wasn't drinking champagne?

ALEXANDER

Well, I'm not a spy or a cop, am I? I'm a curator. A very happy one.

MEL

You haven't complained about your job lately. What's wrong?

ALEXANDER

You're very funny. Shall we go this way?

Alexander pointed to the smaller crater with the distinct view of Devonport and the Waitemata Harbor with Rangitoto, the volcanic cone floating in the hazy distance. They walked single file on the worn track. Other walkers passed going the other way and they stepped aside for the occasional jogger in the fading light. Everyone was polite and gave quick smiles.

.   .   .

On a clear patch of grass ahead, they saw a couple lying on a blanket, a picnic basket spread before them, and what looked like a champagne bottle. The couple laughed, oblivious to the outside world, as they clinked their fluted glasses.

As he got nearer Alexander recognized his old university friend, Nicholas, but could not identify the woman encased in a large maroon kaftan who had her back to him. Nicholas leaped up and walked towards Alexander, his glass in his left hand.

"Nicholas." Alexander caught sight of Tsara on the blanket and froze. She had grown out her pageboy and had a parting on one side. Alexander recovered, turned to Mel, and gave her a quick 'what can I do now?' expression.

"When was the last time we met?" Nicholas shook Alexander's hand.

"Must've been the opening of the Omai Show. With the infamous Captain Cook portrait." He shot a glance at Mel who had kept her distance, her arms folded.

"Oh yes. Wasn't Captain Cook stolen by Māori for a ransom to buy back their land? When you think about it, Captain Cook and Māori land rights, it was a delicious irony."

"Instead, a Soviet spy stole the painting. And I recovered the Captain and exposed a sleeper agent at your university." Alexander saw Tsara was now sitting upright and shooting daggers at him. He ignored her.

"You slept with a Soviet agent?" Nicholas raised his voice.

"No. I exposed; I mean I discovered who she really was. She was related to the actual Soviet spy who had to leave the country. It's a long sordid affair, ultimately it was all about exporting sheep and butter to Moscow. But what about you? Still doing your Ph.D.?"

"It's taking forever. By the way, I'm with Tsara now. You recognize her? She's blossomed with me. Do you want to say hello?"

"I don't think that's a good idea. Tell me about *Tristram Shandy*."

"Your girlfriend's looking a little pissed off, behind you."

Alexander turned to Mel who had stepped back further to admire the view of the harbor.

"Just a minute Mel, then we'll leave."

"Alexander." Nicholas took him by the elbow and led him away from both women. "That's the story about *Tristram Shandy*. There is no story. It's an ebullient celebration of the use of language and the randomness of life. We try to fix the story as a sequence of scenes, no matter how roundabout the characters narrate events. Witness Uncle Toby's famous walking stick passage and the drawing he makes as he waves it around. There's no such phenomenon as a tangential sideline, an off-subject distraction, or circumvented circumlocutions. It's all one long, convoluted story."

"Well, how does that affect your thesis?" Alexander acted enthralled. Mel shot him another angry look.

"It affects my thesis in the biggest possible way because I've discovered the very essence of *Tristram Shandy*. I've distilled the elixir."

Alexander could not hide his sense of bewilderment as he turned first to see Tsara's hostile look then Mel's quick shot at him, again. There was an uncomfortable silence on the grassy ridge on the lower crater of Mt. Eden.

"Come on, Nicholas, tell me. What is it?" His eyes swept across the Waitemata Harbor. It was a broken silver mirror.

"That's just it. It will take my entire thesis to explain what I mean, and in doing that, it will be like rewriting, no, copying the entire text of the novel."

"Then why write your thesis? Why not photocopy the entire book and submit that as your thesis? With a cover note, a short essay explaining, of course."

"You mean like a performance piece? That's not a bad idea. And I take it you're not being your usual sarcastic self?"

Alexander shook his head. "I knew someone who submitted a taped recording of his interview with Stockhausen for his Ph.D. in music. Stockhausen was so taken by someone from New Zealand calling him in the middle of the night at his studio in Germany that he talked for hours. His professor was a fan of Stockhausen, so he got amazing marks, or whatever you call it. All from one night, and my friend never wrote a word. Tell me, Nicholas, is your professor a fan of Laurence Sterne?"

"Alexander. You know it." His eyes were like wheels spinning.

"Well, it was nice bumping into you. Give Tsara my best." They shook hands.

"I understand you have a history with Tsara." Nicholas kept hold of Alexander's hand longer than necessary.

"I'm sure there are at least two different versions." He broke free and walked with Mel back the way they had come until they arrived at another mound. They stopped to admire the lights going on in Devonport and outlines of boats on the Waitemata Harbor.

"If you don't kiss me right now, I'll scream, holler and cry." Mel grabbed Alexander's arm.

"In that order? I thought you'd cry, scream then holler."

Mel glared at Alexander.

"So this isn't going to end like a Chekhov story?"

"Kiss me, you idiot."

It was a long kiss. Rangitoto disappeared in a black curtain of rain. They heard Nicholas's voice.

"We forgot the mayonnaise!"

FORBIDDEN LOVE

She grasped the gear stick with her left hand, a firm grip under the knob. She looked at me with a certain smile, waited a moment, then rammed the car into first, let out the clutch, and accelerated. She looked at me again with the same smile.

I was on the side of the road, north of Hamilton, trying to hitchhike from Wellington to Auckland in one day. The sun was setting, and I didn't want to be stranded on a dark road.

A red sports car had screeched to a halt next to me, and a young woman wound down the passenger window and asked where I was headed. "Auckland. Remuera."

"Jump in."

I jumped in.

We had a moment where we exchanged looks.

She gained speed, a lot of speed. I marveled at her shiny long hair, how she controlled the steering wheel and the way she charged through the gears. Her olive complexion glowed. She smelled of exotic flowers and her blue eyes laughed. She parted her lips and seemed to hold her breath as she gazed at me between negotiating corners and over-taking cars. She kept a firm grasp on her gear stick and made sure I noticed.

I resolved to be on my best behavior for the promised ride to Auckland. I asked questions about her. She asked questions about me. We chatted like old friends.

She drove to my house as if she knew where it was, and I invited her in for a cup of tea. She did not hesitate. She followed me into the empty house I shared with my brother, who was away on a business trip. I never made tea.

Abandoning our inhibitions, we explored and then devoured each other, steeped in pleasure.

Exhausted, we fell asleep in each other's arms and then woke an hour later. We started again, slowly, more considerate, more sensual. Her lips, her hands, her entire body exhibited a serene mastery as if she had been making love for a thousand years and knew every detail, every caress that would thrill and satisfy me.

I imagined there was a deep connection between us that was both exciting and frightening.

At dawn, we lay against each other, and I could not keep my eyes off her sleeping form, as if she was from another world. From my bedroom window, I watched the sunrise over Rangitoto, across the harbor.

Later that morning she got dressed and gave me a long kiss as she lingered over my sprawled body. The kiss was tender, and as she looked into my eyes, and stroked my face, I had a feeling we would never see each other again after such an unforgettable night and she knew this too. She left me her phone number after I asked for it.

I tried calling the next day, but I could never reach her. I tried all week until I realized it was hopeless, and I would never see her again.

For months I struggled to understand what had happened. The most pragmatic explanation was she had picked me up on a whim, a fantasy of hers. We had a one-night stand, then she went back to her prescribed life. The other explanation: she was an angel, and to protect me, we could not see each other again, for such intimacy with a human was prohibited. I preferred the second explanation; however irrational it was.

I did not bathe for days. I wanted to keep her smell on me. I cannot remember her smell now. Nor can I recall her name.

Like the narrator of Vivant Denon's French eighteenth-century masterpiece, *No Tomorrow,* where he had a similar all-night experience, I looked for a moral to this story and found none.

TWO YEARS LATER

In Sydney for the Biennale, I was at a party in a large club. No one was dancing. I spotted a tall blonde wearing a shirt with braces and baggy pants. She stood in the center of what was the dance floor, surrounded by people talking and holding drinks. When she saw me, she fixed me with her blue eyes, as if waiting for me.

I was drinking red wine out of a bottle, and I offered her a drink. She smiled at me and took a long swig.

The party was noisy. We had to shout at each other to make ourselves heard. She called herself Sara, and we formally shook hands. She laughed at the irony of my manners as I offered her another swig of the bottle. Sara said she had to go to an appointment and apologized. She only had one more day in Sydney then was returning to Adelaide. I told her I wanted to spend more time with her and asked for her phone number. We agreed to meet the next night.

Without pen and paper, I repeated the phone number a hundred times. It was the most important number I had ever remembered.

The next day I called Sara, and we arranged to meet at a gallery opening in the late afternoon. I brought my SX-70 camera, and extra boxes of film stuffed into my denim jacket pockets. She appeared at the gallery looking even more radiant with her braces and white shirt and baggy pants. We talked about her pottery and kiln and why I was carrying a Polaroid camera slung over my shoulder. We ate cheese and crackers at the gallery, our dinner. I was more intoxicated being in her presence than from the two glasses of wine. We walked to the waterfront and around a neighborhood of old brick buildings covered in graffiti and looked at the Harbor Bridge from a unique angle. All I could think about was her face, her profile and I stopped to take Polaroids of her. We watched the prints come alive. Having her hair fall over my shoulder and catching her breath was heaven. I gave her the Polaroids.

After a long walk through narrow streets with pioneer cottages, we came to a house I recognized. Friends were about to leave for a party, and they invited us in for a quick drink. We stayed talking in the kitchen after my friends left. They told us we could stay as long as we liked.

Sara's smile made me feel at ease. I could talk to her about anything, and she must have felt the same way. I took more

Polaroids. I could not remember when I last felt so relaxed and excited.

Later, we sat on the sofa in the empty house. I think she was waiting for me to kiss her. I could sense our bodies waiting for greater intimacy. All my inhibitions and fears fell away.

I do not remember who made the first move. We hugged for a long time then drew back and looked into each other's eyes. We did not have to speak to understand what was happening.

All the Polaroids we had taken were displayed on the coffee table in front of us. We both wanted to do art projects with them. I could not tell if time speeded up or stopped.

When light appeared through the window, we were still clothed and held each other. Sara wanted to go upstairs and make love. I did not want to break the spell we were under. I did not know if she was an angel or an ordinary being, although there was nothing ordinary about her.

Looking at her face, her smile, her eyes, I was engulfed for one evening in a cloud of love I could not have imagined.

Sara had to catch a morning train to Adelaide, and she did not want me to go to the train station. I did not ask for her address or phone number there, and she did not ask for mine.

I escorted her to a taxi.

She disappeared from my life with the Polaroids.

I tried to discover why I was fated to spend a magical night with such an extraordinary woman. Again, I thought of the narrator of Vivant Denon's *No Tomorrow*, who had a similar, though far more physical, all-night experience. He sought meaning to what had happened to him, but he could find none.

I did know Sara disrupted my life for a long time and disturbed my relationships with other women, none of whom could ever match her beauty, her serenity, her easy and loving presence. When I returned to New Zealand, I could not reconcile what had happened in Sydney, being with a woman named Sara. I was on the verge several times of dropping everything to rush to Adelaide to find her, but I knew she would not be there.

All I had left were a handful of Polaroids. I could not stop looking at them.

All photographs are in the public domain or owned and copyrighted by the author unless indicated.

Front cover Polaroid by the author.

Amanda, St Francis, Goya, Joni Mitchell and Ma Bell
Stamp showing Francisco Goya's *Nude Maja.*

An Eighteen Century Love Problem
An Interesting Problem by Adolphe Alexandre Lesrel (1839–1929).

Daisy Crown
Photo by author

A Love Story about a Fortunate Book
Photos of the discarded book by the author.

Nikolai Nikolaevich and Anna Sergeyevna, Sibling Love, Moscow Style
The order of Lenin medal. Private collection.

Mel comes to the Mountain or Chekhov and Mayonnaise
Rangitoto and the Waitemata Harbor from the lower crater on top of Mount Eden, now called Maungawhau – photo by author

Portrait of Anton Pavlovich Chekhov, 1898 by Osip Braz.

Forbidden Love
Garden statue by author.
Polaroid by author.

Nick Spill portrait in his office by Frank Miranda.

Nick Spill photo before the pandemic by Joy Spill.

Left: Nick Spill – in his office. Right: Nick Spill – before the pandemic.

Nick Spill graduated from the University of Auckland. He became an Exhibitions Curator at the National Art Gallery in New Zealand and moved to the US in 1980 on an Arts Council grant.

Spill formed a Private Investigation Agency in Miami and later become Chief Investigator for a State Agency. He authored *The Way of the Bodyguard* about his years as a bodyguard and investigator and co-wrote his father's Burma war memoir *Reluctant Q*. He contributed to the N.Z. best-selling compilation, *Grumpy Old Men 2*.

He completed *The Jaded Trilogy: The Jaded Kiwi, The Jaded Spy*, and *The Jaded Widow*, dark crime novels with an off-beat humor, set in New Zealand in the mid-1970s.

On returning from a lecture he delivered at the Auckland Art Gallery, about Conceptual Art in New Zealand in the 1970s, he wrote the illustrated essay, *Reflections on the TranzAlpine: Kiwis, Art, Death, Coffee, Sex.*

He wrote *The Sense of Blood Ink, Nine Stories about Love*, during the global pandemic. He is currently working on another love story.

More information is available at: https://nickspill.com